# pass it on

**15+**

# pass it on

## j.minter

BLOOMSBURY

**BLOOMSBURY**

First published in Great Britain in 2005 by Bloomsbury Publishing Plc
38 Soho Square, London, W1D 3HB

Produced by Alloy Entertainment
151 West 26th Street
New York, NY 10001

A CIP catalogue record of this book is available
from the British Library

ISBN 0 7475 7474 X

All papers used by Bloomsbury Publishing are natural, recyclable
products made from wood grown in well-managed forests. The
manufacturing processes conform to the environmental regulations of
the country of origin.

Printed in Great Britain by Clays Ltd, St Ives plc

10 9 8 7 6 5 4 3 2 1

for SKS

**a word or two from your good friend jonathan,**
**the social glue**

The other day I was walking down Ninth Street, headed over to Patch's, and this girl with honey-colored hair and a long, gray coat passed by me. We smiled at each other, because we'd definitely been at parties together. This was before all the secrets around me started to churn, just a few weeks before Thanksgiving.

The streets of New York City shone in the sunlight and the wind was strong. Brightly colored leaves rustled in the wind. In the fall, I like to have a warm, dark-colored sweater on hand—either for me, or to lend to a girl like that, like the one in the long, gray coat who walked by me that day and who shared the trace of a smile.

I remember looking at that girl and wondering, *what's her secret?* Then, only a few days later, when all the secrets started to build, they felt like the big difference between me and my friends.

Whenever I saw a girl, or even other guys, I thought, *what's their secret?* And I wondered that about people because all of a sudden I had so many secrets of my own.

Now I believe that everybody I like has secrets. They sprout up fresh all the time, like mushrooms or something growing in nature that I'm not familiar with, since I rarely leave Manhattan.

But let's start this story right at the moment when I had to take on my first big secret, which is about my dad and what he'd been up to over in London, where he moved about five years ago when he left my mom and me and my brother.

This is the secret that I had to keep from everyone. And I'm pretty sure it's the one that set all the others in motion. Soon enough the secrets were growing, gaining speed, and rushing toward me and my friends until we had no choice—we had to either knock them apart or let them mow us all down. And that girl I saw on Ninth Street? Yeah, I got to see her again.

# a cool shiver of a saturday, the snap of thanksgiving in the air

### who knew the apartment needed
### a fresh coat of paint?

"I can't believe it," I said. "Dad's getting remarried next week and we find out now?" I leaned
against the doorway of my brother Ted's bedroom. My mother was in the hallway, facing me.

"I understand that this might be upsetting for
you, Jonathan."

"Might?" My foot jumped suddenly as if the
ground below it had gotten overheated. "Have
you called Ted?" I asked.

"I left him a message." My mother inspected
the yellow-white wall. The paint was cracked and
flaking in places. She smiled and nodded to herself. "In any case, the important thing for you to
know is that I'm taking a vacation, and while I'm
gone, we're having the apartment painted."

"We? Are you sure this is really necessary?"

She'd been threatening to do this for a while.
We live in this gigantic rambler of an apartment

on Fifth Avenue and Eleventh Street, on the eleventh floor, and sometimes I feel like the apartment is prehistoric or something—like it's always been there—which is why I got so weirded out when my mom said she was going to change something about it. My mouth hung open. I stared down at my new Prada loafers, but I found no solace there. I looked back and my mom was still looking at me.

"I'm quite sure. This place will be an uninhabitable mess for a couple weeks. So you can either stay in a hotel or spend a few days with each of your friends."

"Where are you going?" I asked. Maybe it's because my brother's up at Vassar, or because I'm practically halfway through my junior year, but my mom seems to feel that most of the time I can pretty much take care of myself.

"I'm flying to Paris tomorrow night." She smiled at me. "Milla is still there and she's going to take care of me."

"What about Thanksgiving?"

"Oh, I'll be back before then."

"But it's next Thursday."

"Is it? I'll tell my travel agent."

"Well, I guess I'll just shuttle between my

friends' houses," I said.

"You can stop by here during the day, but all the furniture is being moved out tomorrow morning. With your dislike of disorder, darling, you can see why you should go elsewhere." She moved into the living room and I followed.

I didn't even bother to start getting annoyed with her about how this was going to affect my schoolwork or how she could've maybe waited till December break. I got that there was a reason why she was cleaning house and flying to Paris to be taken care of by her best friend from college. She was upset because my dad had called to say he was going to get remarried. He's a real piece of work, my dad. If he didn't send the checks that kept me and my brother in school and my mom in couture clothes from Bergdorf's, our opinion of him would've fallen so low years ago that by now we'd have completely lost track of it.

"How'd he deliver the news?"

"He called last night. Her name is long, but I wrote it down: Penelope Isquierdo Santana Suttwilley."

"PISS?" I asked.

My mother laughed, and her right eye began to blink uncontrollably.

"Why, yes. I've heard from Arno's father, Alec, that she looks a lot like me. She's younger of course, and probably spunkier. Apparently Alec Wildenburger is going to be the best man."

"Uh-huh."

"Alec said it will be a small ceremony, with only a few of their closest friends. I'm sure your father is going to call you, he just hasn't had a chance yet."

She brushed my hair off my forehead and walked back down the hall toward her bedroom. She was putting an earring on, so she listed to the left. I closed my eyes and tried to imagine a different, better color for our apartment walls. But I couldn't. Everything was fine the way it was. And who cares about wall paint anyway? Not me, and I'm exactly the sort of detail-oriented person who is supposed to.

I went back into my bedroom and sat down in the chair at my desk. It was about noon, and the sun was starting to shine through the clouds. I'd hung out with my guys last night—first at Patch's, and then we'd all gone over to Mickey's girlfriend Philippa's house until really late, because her parents were in Long Island—but I hadn't talked to anyone yet that day, so I called Arno's cell.

"Arno's cell. Liesel speaking." She pronounced it *Awww-no's*.

"Oh, hi. Could I talk to Arno?"

There was muffled laughter. Then Arno got on the line.

"She slept over?" I asked.

"Yeah. My parents don't know she's here. What's up?"

I gulped some air. Arno had only just met Liesel the night before—she was a very "uptown" girl Philippa knew from school and she'd arrived at like three in the morning. I'd barely shaken hands with her. But I guess Arno had made a much stronger connection. Through the phone, I could hear the new Beastie Boys CD playing. I punched up the same sounds on my iPod.

"Look dude, I need to stay at your place for a couple of days. My mom's having our apartment painted."

"Cool. The Rentmeesters are upstairs in the penthouse, but you can stay in my room. This starts when?"

"Tomorrow night?"

"Yeah, come by for dinner—you'd have probably done that anyway. Ow!"

Arno ended the call. Though I knew next to nothing about Liesel, I figured that a girl who could take center stage in Arno's life so quickly probably wasn't the type to wait patiently for him to get off the phone. As I set down the receiver, I wondered if Arno's dad had told him about my dad and PISS yet. I would have called him back to ask, but I had a feeling Leisel wouldn't let him answer, so I decided to skip it.

I stood up and looked around my bedroom, which was spare and clean. The only things I keep around are a lot of music, my clothes (evenly spaced on a steel rack), and a desk that I sit at while I make my phone calls. I kind of love my room. It's minimal, but very "rock" at the same time. Very "rich punk," which is how I've been feeling lately.

"Jonathan, we're going to paint your room too," my mom yelled.

I immediately got up and went down the hall to her bedroom. "Can I ask why?" I asked.

"Because I think we need a change, that's why."

She was packing and speaking in French to her friend Milla. Her French is more than a little grating.

"No!" I heard her say. "He's using the wedding to come clean about his past? He can't!" She turned toward the wall and leaned her head against it, which was not the kind of thing I'd ever seen my mom do before. She ended the call and looked at me. "I need you home tonight," she said. "Your father is trying to turn over a new leaf. May God help us all!"

"Why does that mean I have to be home?"

"Well . . . because if your father does call, I want you to talk to him. There's more going on here than just the marriage or the paint and I feel it'd be best for him to tell you. Obviously if Alec Wildenburger is his best man, then he doesn't have any idea what's really going on."

I looked at her, puzzled. "What are you talking about, Mom?"

"Nothing, dear. Maybe it's nothing." She scratched at her hand, which is something she does when she's nervous. "In any case, I'm having dinner tonight with the Grobarts, but you'll stay home for the call, won't you?"

"*Oh-kaaay*," I said. "Then I'm going to rent some movies." A Saturday night at home wasn't necessarily a bad thing—Friday night had definitely been wild enough that somebody might want to just come over and hang out and watch movies or whatever.

"In the meantime, there's one other thing you should know. The painter is starting Monday morning. You remember Gerald and Gina Shanlon? That artistic couple we shared the beach house in Sag Harbor with when you were six? The Always Nakeds, your father and I called them. Remember their son, Billy? He's going to be staying here and painting the house. If you do happen to stop by to pick up clothes or something, you might run into him."

"Did you tell him to be extra careful in my room?"

"Sure I did—" But her telephone was ringing, and it was probably someone with more gossip about my dad. I threw on my jean jacket and went down to the street to get some food and rent some DVDs—I was definitely up for seeing *Eternal Sunshine* again. And I figured I'd make my walk a long one, because if there was one thing that would take my mind off whatever seemed to be happening, it was the chance of running into that girl with the honey-colored hair and the warm smile.

"What'd you do last night?" Arno Wildenburger asked. He sat back in one of Patch Flood's gigantic white beanbag chairs.

"Went over and watched movies at Jonathan's house," Patch said. He stood on a skateboard in the middle of his room in the Floods' town house on Perry Street. It was Sunday afternoon, and they'd been watching football, but the Giants were losing by so much that they'd had to turn it off.

Arno was kind of psyched to be hanging out with Patch—he needed a rest from Liesel, whom he'd been with for thirty-six hours straight. He felt pretty lucky to have caught Patch at home.

"Did anybody else come over? Liza Komansky?" Arno asked.

"Nope, it was just us. Apparently she's still annoyed with Jonathan about their friendship."

"Because they can't be friends since she has a crush on him?"

"I think that was it," Patch said. "And she definitely

still has that crush. She's always talking about it at school—to the point where even *I* heard about it."

Patch went to Turner, a private coed school in the West Village. And since Arno and Jonathan both went to Gissing, which was all boys, they always wanted to know about girls from Turner. David went to Potterton, which was all boys, too. And Mickey went to Adele Biggs, on the Upper West Side, which was coed and cool and all, but populated mostly by super-privileged burnouts and problem children who'd been kicked out of boarding schools for drugs and bad attitudes.

Patch smiled the wide, gleeful smile that made people compare him to sports stars like Beckham and actors like Brad Pitt—guys who were always winning and looked really happy.

"Hey did I tell you? I ended up kissing Selina Trieff on Friday night."

"What about Graca?"

"Graca's twenty-three. She never wanted to just skateboard around under the Brooklyn Bridge or get high and hang out at Sheep's Meadow."

"I get that." Arno nodded. "Jonathan's going to stay at my house for a couple of days. His mom's getting their apartment painted."

"Yeah, he told me." Patch had his eyes closed and he

was listening to the music, swaying back and forth on the board. He was barefoot. His khakis were hanging halfway off his ass and he didn't have a shirt on. "I think some stuff's going on with him."

"Like what?" Arno picked up a Pomona College catalog that was on the floor.

"Dunno. He said he was waiting for a call from his dad, but he didn't really go into it."

"So, what's Selina Trieff like anyway?" Arno asked.

"Selina? She's—" Patch paused. Arno watched him. He couldn't describe Selina either. She was quiet and not very flirty. On weekends she mostly stayed out at her parents' mansion in Oyster Bay. That kind of girl baffled Arno.

"Selina's cool. I think I'm going to see her later. What about you? What happened with that uptown girl, Liesel Reid?"

"I've been hanging out with her since the last time I saw you," Arno said.

"Well?" Patch asked.

"We're like soul mates, and I think it might be freaking me out."

"You sound scared, dude."

"She's a little—" Arno paused, and began the slow search for the right word. "What Jonathan calls people that remind him of himself: pretentious. But she's really, really fun."

"So?" Patch asked. "That should work for you. You're the most pretentious guy I know."

Before Arno could decide if he were annoyed or not and then respond accordingly, someone knocked hard on the door and swung it open.

"David for you," Patch's little sister, Flan Flood, said. She was in her riding outfit, complete with crop and velvet helmet, which she'd begun to wear around the house obsessively. Arno stared at her. Although she seemed nice enough, he had no idea why Jonathan had been so drawn to her—but this was mostly because she was in eighth grade and way too shy to speak directly to Arno. She banged off down the hall without another word.

"Hey." David ducked into Patch's room. Arno and Patch nodded at David, who threw himself down on a yellow chair shaped like a paint blob that had somehow made its way into Patch's room along with loads of other assorted family junk.

David sighed. He was in his standard oversized jeans and blue hooded Yale sweatshirt that had been personally sent to him by the Yale basketball coach. He was about six foot four and handsome, with a big hawk-nose and black hair that he was currently wearing in an outdated and messy David Schwimmer-like crew cut.

"Have you seen Jonathan?" David asked.

"Not yet today," Patch said.

David shrugged. "My parents were out with Jonathan's mom last night. My dad says there's some thing with her that's an emergency."

"Patch just told me that Jonathan was freaking out last night," Arno said.

Patch stopped rocking on his skateboard. "I did not say that."

"My dad says something went wrong with his dad," David said. "But then he got started talking about all this other stuff and I tuned him out after that."

The three friends were quiet for a moment. Outside, the crackling November wind was blowing hard and could be heard under the music, so Patch switched over to the new Ebony Eyes CD and turned it up.

Then they heard Flan scream. They all looked at each other and nodded.

"Mickey," Arno said, staring into a mirror, arching one perfect eyebrow, and then the other.

"Fuck you!" Flan screamed. There was a popping noise, of what must have been her riding helmet bouncing down the stairs.

"Your stupid friend is here," Flan announced from the hall.

"She's getting cuter by the minute," Mickey said as

24

he came into Patch's room. "Jonathan was right about her."

"What do you mean?" Patch asked.

"Forget it," Arno said quickly.

Mickey was in a black and silver tracksuit. He'd cut off his blond tips and now his thick hair was nearly an Afro, with corkscrews shooting off in all directions. His goggles dangled around his neck along with a ring of keys to his parents' various houses. His mother had him wearing a beeper now. Ever since he'd tried to eat a freshman a few weeks ago, and nearly gotten himself kicked out of school, his parents were keeping him on a much tighter leash. He was still allowed to go out with Philippa Frady, though. They were still in love.

"Bleeah!" Mickey said, and fell on David.

"Hey you nitwits," Flan yelled from downstairs. "Mom and Dad said to eat without them. They're not coming back from Connecticut after all."

"Mmm. Let's get Jonathan and go over to Odeon for some fried chicken," Patch said, and started to look for a phone.

"Sounds good," Arno said. He stood up.

Suddenly, there was a ringing noise from under a pile of dirty jeans. Patch started to dig. Then the noise stopped.

"Patch!" Flan yelled. "It's Selina for you!"

"He's with that shy Selina Trieff now," Arno said to David.

"Wow, I wonder what that's like," David said.

"They're probably all quiet together—I bet they barely even talk."

"Like the opposite of me and Amanda." David's beeper went off. It was Amanda. He rummaged through his schoolbag to find his cell so he could call her.

Mickey and Arno stared at each other.

"Mickey!"

Even though the room was loud with music, they could hear Philippa Frady yelling from her town house across the yard from Patch's. Mickey and Arno looked over. She was waving. She was a tall girl with a loud voice and she always looked extremely prim—now she was wearing a long black skirt and a white sweater— but everyone knew she was kind of crazy underneath it all, which was why she loved Mickey.

"My parents still haven't come back," she yelled.

"I better get over there." Mickey nodded to Patch and David, who were both on the phone. "Tell them I said 'later.'"

Mickey made his way down the stairs. Arno turned and listened to his other two friends as they made plans with their girlfriends. So Arno called Liesel.

"Arno," Liesel said. "How'd you know to call? You must have ESB. Come uptown right now. We're planning a Monday night party and we could use a little downtown flair." Which she pronounced *fleah*. She was originally from Germany and often said she missed it terribly. Arno was still a bit awed by her. She went to Nightingale, was stinking rich, and was generally considered to be the most beautiful sixteen-year-old girl in the city, if not the state, and probably, therefore, the country. Except L.A., which didn't count.

"Okay." Arno ended the call with her and turned to his guys. But David had already left for Amanda's and Patch was looking around for a shirt so he could get over to Selina Trieff's house.

"Let's all hang out later this week," Arno said as he left the house with Patch, who'd given up on the idea of a shirt. Apparently finding a clean one was just too complicated.

"Definitely." Patch dropped his board on the sidewalk and stepped on. "I'll call Jonathan and make sure he arranges it."

### i get some really good, and some very bad, news

Early on Sunday evening, I finished packing the bag I planned to take to Arno's. My mom was still puttering around, waiting for her car to drive her to the eight p.m. flight to Paris. I figured that when she left I would too, since the painter was coming at seven the next morning and I had no reason not to get myself over to Arno's. I checked again through my things—my fall sweaters and the several pairs of shoes I'd fit into red felt bags.

Patch had called in the afternoon to say that we should all get together soon, and I could hear in his voice that he was worried about me, or something. My dad hadn't called the night before when he was over, but I'd told him about my dad and PISS anyway. I knew Patch wouldn't tell anyone before I did, and I really appreciated that about him.

"I've got a good idea!" My mom practically

ran into my room. "You'll come with me in the car out to Kennedy, and then drive back to the city. That way we'll have some time to talk."

"That'll take two hours."

"It'll be fun! And I was sorry I didn't get to see you more yesterday."

"You were out at dinner with the Grobarts from six till midnight."

"And that's part of why we need to talk now, because dear old Sam Grobart really helped me see some things—"

The phone rang then. I assumed it was the car company saying that her car was downstairs, so I answered it "Talk to me," which I knew my mom hated.

"Jonathan?"

I froze. It was my dad. "Hey. Um, sorry about that. I thought you were the car service."

"Nah, just me, son." Since moving to London, my dad had developed an unfortunate faux British accent, like Madonna. It killed me. "How are you?"

"Fine, Dad. You?"

We went on like that for a minute while my mom wandered around my room and took a seat on my bed, watching me, which was weird. I congratulated him on PISS, though I didn't call her that, and still felt I had to turn away from my mom when I said it.

"Jonathan, there are some things I'd like to tell you. The first is that you'll soon have a stepbrother. His name is Serge. He's your age and very cool. He's like you in a way, only a bit taller. Anyway, he's going to join Penelope and me on our honeymoon next month." I made a face at my mom like Dad was being totally nuts, but he kept talking. "Penelope is incredibly wealthy."

"Great, Dad." My voice was flat.

"She has a boat, a yacht, a ship, whatever you call these two-hundred-fifty-foot sailing monstrosities. The crew is bringing it from the Mediterranean to the States right now, and after Christmas we're taking it from Miami, through the Caribbean, to Venezuela to visit Penelope's family. We'd like you to join us as well."

"Um, well, I can't really sail." Other than saying, *no fucking way am I bunking with a weird kid named Serge in the middle of the ocean,* this seemed like the most legit excuse.

"Not relevant. There's a sixteen-man crew, incredible food, and all the luxuries of a five-star hotel. You won't have to worry about a thing, unless you feel like joining Serge for the waterfall hikes in Venezuela, of course." He chuckled like that was a really hilarious image, which, of course, it was. "It would mean a lot to me, Jonathan."

I paused. Something was off here. "Dad, what's going on? There's something else. I can tell." I said it with more authority than I felt, which was probably good, since I wasn't nearly strong enough to hear all the things I was about to start hearing.

He made an uncomfortable noise. "Yes, Jonathan, there's more. You're right, but I don't think you need to hear it from me. Your mother has always been better at this type of thing. I think she should tell you."

"This is kind of freaking me out." The "out" got caught in my throat, and I made a clearing sound like it itched, even though I knew that wasn't the problem.

"Just remember, Jonathan, it's not about the money." I heard him cover the phone for a second with his hand and say something to someone with a twittery voice that I could only imagine was PISS. "And you can bring one of your friends. I'd say bring them all, but even a few hundred feet can get crowded in the middle of the Caribbean. And buy the clothes that you'll need for the trip, too. You have the AmEx, son."

It occurred to me as I hung up the phone that I didn't exactly want my dad calling me "son" right then, even if it was attached to a shopping spree. Not until I knew what the hell was going on, at least. I turned back to face my mom, who was still on my bed.

"Did he tell you, sweetheart?"

My mom never said things like "sweetheart," so I started to really panic. "He told me he's taking me on a huge yacht and that I could bring one friend and that you would tell me the rest."

The phone rang again, and I answered it with a normal greeting, even though this time it was the car company after all.

"Just come with me darling—there's nowhere better to talk than in the back of a cozy black town car."

"Fine," I said, not sure what else to do.

So we zipped up our bags and made a last-minute check of the apartment. We went and got into the elevator with old Richard, the elevator guy.

"Big paint job coming," Richard said mournfully, like a paint job was a hurricane, or a blackout.

"Yes. Sorry about that," my mom said.

"I guess nothing can be done now." Richard sighed. My mother rolled her eyes at me.

In the lobby, Richard helped us get our bags into the back of the town car. My mom's driver had quit a few weeks before to start a Brazilian restaurant on the Lower East Side, so we'd been using a service. This driver had a shaved head and wore a headset. He barely looked at us. We clambered into the back and then my mother turned to face me.

"So there's more?" I asked. The car was warm, but it also smelled strongly of cologne. I tried to open the window, but it didn't work. We drove toward Houston Street, but the traffic was heavy. So we sat there, only two blocks from our house, in traffic. "Look, can I just get out? I'm going to be late for dinner at the Wildenburgers."

My mother brushed at the air in front of her. "Don't be ridiculous. This is far more important. Frankly, I wish you didn't have to know, but here we are." She stopped talking and looked out the window at a guy passing by on a bicycle.

"Mom?"

"Right, yes. So, your father seems to have chosen the occasion of his upcoming wedding to come clean about a few things."

"That's bad?"

"It isn't good. When we were all younger, back when you and your friends were schoolmates at Grace Church Elementary, your father helped everyone with their taxes. He was a true wiz with a tax form. Perhaps we should've been suspicious even then . . ."

"I thought he was an accountant."

"He became a sort of investment counselor. And he lost great sums of money for all of his clients. At least, that was how it appeared."

"But he earned it back, right? I mean, he's got a lot of money now, doesn't he?"

"He also lost money for the Wildenburgers and the Pardos and the Floods and the Grobarts. Sam Grobart and I had a long session before we went out for dinner last night. If he weren't my therapist, I don't know what I'd do. It was his suggestion that I be open and honest with you about all this, even if your father isn't."

"Come on, Mom, even David admits that his dad is crazy. I thought you knew that!"

"That's wholly untrue. The man's a genius.

Anyway, years ago we thought everything your father did was perfectly legal. And then he and I divorced. And he fled to London."

"Yeah. I've seen him like twice since then."

"Yes, well, he's done a poor job of being in touch with any of us. But his checks have always arrived on time. Now your father has admitted that he didn't lose all of that money after all. Apparently, he made it look as though he'd made some bad investments, but really, he stole the money."

I made a little throttling sound in my throat. "From who?" I asked, even though I already knew the answer.

"From everyone, darling—the Floods, the Pardos, the Grobarts, the Wildenburgers. Others, too, it seems."

I stared at the headrest in front of me, not saying anything.

"We'll need each other's help through this period, Jonathan. I'd ask your brother to come home, but to be honest, I've always found him a little remote. Of course you'll need counseling. This will not be easy."

"How can we help each other if you're going to Paris? And aren't you pissed at Dad?"

"Well, yes I'm extremely—"

I pulled at the door-lock. We were near the Williamsburg Bridge, but we weren't on it yet. I could still get out of the car and be in Manhattan.

"But this was all a long time ago. Jonathan, do you understand? Everything is different now."

"How?"

My mother stared straight in front of her at the back of the driver's head, which had grown redder as he listened to our strange family tale. Immediately I hoped he didn't drive for any of my friends' families.

"Dad said it wasn't about the money . . ." I trailed off.

"The hell it's not." She sighed. "But if this Penelope is so rich, perhaps that should take care of some things."

"I think I'm going to get out of the car now."

"Sam Grobart says you can go and talk to him if you want."

"Yeah, that'll happen."

She touched my cheek, which I let her do since she is my mother, after all. "You should still go on that boat trip. This, too, shall pass."

I pecked at her cheek, zipped up my jacket, and got out. The trunk opened and I grabbed my bag and gently pushed it shut. I could feel my mom's eyes on me as I tried to decide which direction to go. My eyes were smarting and I wiped at them. After a moment of indecision, I headed northwest, in the direction of Arno's house. I figured I'd walk for a while and then grab a cab.

But I slowed down. *Wait.* If Mr. Grobart knew all about what happened—that my dad had stolen bundles of money from him and from all my friends' families—and if he'd talked to my mom about it, would that mean David knew?

I walked quickly along Delancey, back toward the West Village. I passed McDonald's and Burger King and Sneakerworld and Sneakerhaven. Usually if I was this far east, it was past midnight and I was with my guys, but right now it wasn't even totally dark out. I turned to look behind me at the stream of cars going over the bridge. I hoped my mom would be okay. I hoped her friend Milla would help her out.

And then I hitched my bag over my shoulder and put my head down and got going, walking fast, with the hope that I'd get to Arno's with enough time to chill out and forget all this and maybe get some homework done before dinner.

## arno is in the bright, burning beginning of a very wild relationship

Arno was at Liesel's house, playing music and fooling around with her.

"You fucking stud," Liesel said. She was in his lap. Arno stared at her. He smiled, and hoped his look suggested that people should only say things like that as a joke, even though she wasn't kidding. They were drinking leftover champagne from the fridge and eating some square-cut sandwiches they'd found on a silver tray in the kitchen.

"You're so into it." Arno tried to sound gruff, but he didn't even know what he meant by it. He just couldn't think of what else to say.

"Yeah," Liesel roared at him. She was certainly a knockout. She was nearly six feet tall—exactly as tall as, if not a bit taller than, Arno. She had practically no hips and very small breasts. But her eyes were huge and blue and she had a thick mane of ash-blond hair. Her voice was almost as deep as Arno's and she had a tendency to swallow and then roll her *r*'s, so she could be both loud and a little bit hard to understand. Any way he looked at it, she freaked him out.

After he met her on Friday night, they'd spent all day Saturday in bed. And then, once it was Saturday night, they went slumming at the 40/40 Club and ended up making out in a bathroom stall. Then he'd gotten away from her for those two good hours at Patch's and now he was back. And it was only now, in her house, that he realized her parents were *the* Reids, well-known art collectors. Of course, his parents were well-known art dealers. They were dangerously well matched.

"Let's watch repeats of that stupid *Newlyweds* show!" she yelled. Arno practically had to cover his ears. She stood up, shirtless, and bounded out of the room, toward her bedroom.

"I'll be there in a second." Arno looked around. Liesel's parents were at a dinner party so Arno and Liesel had been hanging out in the formal living room, which was covered with an amazing variety of printed fabrics. There were all sorts of flowers: real ones in vases, a flower print on the wallpaper, and raised ones in velvet on the couch. Downtown, nobody ever bothered covering everything with weird colors that way. It was giving him a headache. Arno's phone rang and the screen lit up with the words *MEAN OLD LADY*.

"Hi, Mom."

"No, it's me, Jonathan. I'm at your house."

"Oh. Right. I'll be home soon, dude."

"Hurry up!" Liesel screamed.

"Okay, take your time," Jonathan said. Arno clicked off. Jonathan sounded weirdly quiet and awkward, and Arno thought about what Patch and David had said about something being up with him.

"I'll watch the show with you, but then I have to go home," Arno said to Liesel.

"Fuck that!" He heard her scream. She had the TV on loud. She did everything loud. They hadn't had sex yet, but Arno was sure it would be sonic-boom loud. He was a little afraid they'd tear apart whatever room they used. He wanted to get her to his parents' new place on Shelter Island, where nobody could hear them, but he wasn't sure he could handle another entire weekend with her. He already felt like he needed to sleep for a couple of days to recover from this one.

"Come on baby!" she yelled.

Arno stood up. He sucked air in through his teeth. He caught a glimpse of himself in a silver-framed mirror. His black hair was standing on end and his eyes flashed. He could handle Liesel. She was wild. She was unbelievably beautiful. He was wild. He was painfully good-looking. It fit. He shot out of the living room and made it to her room in a flash—before he could have any more annoying interior thoughts.

**i learn some things that i so do not**
**want to know**

I got off the phone with Arno, who clearly knew nothing about my new predicament, which was a big relief. I still hadn't figured out how I was going to tell my guys that my dad had stolen money from their families, and I definitely wasn't looking forward to it. Obviously my mom was right and there was no way Arno's parents knew the whole story about my dad, since Arno's dad was supposedly going to be his best man. I mean, you wouldn't be best man for a guy who'd stolen your money, right?

After one of the kitchen staff had let me into the apartment, I went straight to Arno's room, since I definitely couldn't deal with sussing out who knew what right then. Sitting at Arno's desk, I heard Alec Wildenburger say he was going off somewhere and Mrs. Wildenburger, Allie, tell someone she'd be in her bedroom if they needed her.

When everything seemed quiet and I figured the coast was clear, I wandered down the long hall that separated Arno's bedroom and bathroom from the rest of the house. I was famished and wanted to grab some of the food that was inevitably leftover from whatever event the Wildenburgers had hosted lately. Arno's parents were always hosting events since they lived in a double-wide town house on Eighteenth Street near Tenth Avenue and liked to show it off. For some reason, I kept hoping there'd be leftover chicken legs.

The hall was dark, even though it was just eight o'clock. I crept by the Wildenburgers' bedroom. I knew that Allie was dressing to go out for the evening and that Arno had been wrong—there was no big Sunday meal planned at the Wildenburger house.

"Oh, Ricardo," she said, in her high, wheedling voice. "Stop it."

I stopped. Ricardo was probably Ricardo Pardo, Mickey's father.

"Yes, of course I'm alone."

Weird. I had been over at the Pardos' a million times and never seen Ricardo on the phone. Sometimes he'd throw a phone on the floor to kick it, but I'd never seen him put one to his ear and talk into it. Maybe this was some other Ricardo.

"I can't wait till you're on top of me," Allie said, "you magnificently hot, bearded man!"

Nope. That was Mickey's dad all right. My eyes rolled up in my head. I stepped to my left. The floorboard creaked. I went still.

"Don't talk about Alec," Allie said. "It is impossible being married to a man who won't admit he's gay. He's going to dinner with some man from the Department of Justice—goodness knows why."

I heard the front door lock jangle, fifty feet to my right. I moved quickly, but not before I'd heard more.

"Oh, Ricardo, I can't believe I'm saying this, but I wish he'd find a man and leave me already. And then you and I can finally be really, truly together."

The front door banged open and there was an explosion of bright light down the hall.

"Hello!" Arno screamed out.

I was at the door before Arno could turn his head to look for me.

"What's up?" Arno sounded beat, but happy

to see me. "I always scream hello when I come in so the monsters will know I'm here."

"Why?"

"If I don't, they'll just keep yelling at each other and I'll have to hear some ugly shit I'd be more than happy to not know about, you know?"

"Yes. I know exactly what you mean."

We went into the kitchen. Arno flipped the lights on. He threw his jacket on a chair and went over to the fridge. The room was huge, with loads of gleaming copper pots on hooks and glass-paned cabinets lit from within.

"I think there's some leftover chicken legs." Arno started to push around some white cardboard containers in the fridge.

"You must be reading my mind. How's Liesel?"

"What's all that stuff you like to call somebody when you figure they're probably crazy?" Arno was always asking me for language that way—he could never be bothered to make up his own slang.

"Gingko-biloba? Totally wacked? Nutballs? Whoppers with a side of poppers?"

"Yeah. All that is what she is. She's absolutely incredible, but there's no way I can keep up this thing with her. It's exhausting." Arno sighed happily. He snagged a bottle of Stella Artois from the fridge and cracked it. He said, "I guess I could have worse problems." He paused and took a long sip from his Stella, eyeing me. "What's going on with you, man? You seem, you know, spooked."

I looked down for a minute at the old-school Adidas sneakers I'd put on before I left my house. There was a lot I needed to say, and I knew that right then was the time to say it. "Well, a lot of shit is going on all of a sudden."

"Yeah, I kind of heard that. What's up?"

I opened the fridge and grabbed a bottle of Stella, too. "I just found out my dad's getting remarried to a woman named PISS—Penelope Isquierdo something, something."

Arno's mom walked in and looked at our beers but didn't say anything. "Were you just saying something about Penelope Isquierdo Santana Suttwilley, Jonathan?"

"Um, yeah. She's marrying my dad, but I guess you knew that?"

"Oh, it's hard to keep track of Penelope. But your father is a lucky man, Jonathan. Penelope makes the rest of us look like paupers." She said this while motioning around at their house, which was as big as a mansion in the suburbs and probably worth ten times as much.

"My dad invited me to go on their honeymoon with them through the Caribbean on her two-hundred-fifty-foot sailboat." I looked at Arno and tried to think how I could possibly segue this conversation into *by the way, my dad stole a bunch of money from your family.* And then, maybe because I felt so guilty, I said, "Maybe you can come, too. I think I can bring one friend."

"Abso-fucking-lutely." Arno smiled his big handsome smile and I knew I'd just done something really stupid. What about my other guys?

"Language, Arno," said Allie, but she was already on her way back to her room, so he hardly looked up.

I paused for a second, since I could feel already that these secrets were starting to snowball. I had to tell him.

"Arno, I've got to tell you some—" but instead of going on, I stopped. I couldn't do it. I mean, what if he never had to know? If Penelope was so rich, then maybe this really would just all go away, and I could go on this trip with my dad, and he'd quietly give the money back, and I'd pretend

I never knew about all this awful stuff . . .

"If you were going to tell me I should go to a party Liesel's hosting uptown tomorrow night even though she makes me crazy, then I should tell you that you're right, because that's what's happening."

"I wasn't—"

"What?"

"Wasn't I—nothing," I said.

"Apparently her friends think Monday night is party night."

"Well, so do we."

## david's sweet and somewhat-too-serious
## love affair

"I just hope we're enough for each other," Amanda Harrison Deutschmann said.

"We totally are," David said. "We've been over this. You did something wrong with Arno and I did some bad stuff too, but all that's over."

"I just wish I felt more sure about that," she said and pressed her forehead against her windowpane.

They were in her big room in her family's Tribeca loft, decorated in a mix of what Amanda thought was cool now, which was beige late-sixties furniture, and what she'd thought was cool when she was ten, which was white wood and wicker. There were photos on the walls of Amanda with her friends, and a framed picture of John F. Kennedy Jr. surrounded by clouds.

Amanda had been trying on clothes for the party Liesel Reid was having the next night. The girls knew each other from Nightingale.

"You never used to be so . . . so confident-sounding." Amanda stood in front of him in a purple and pink flowered bra and panties from La Petite Coquette. Her parents were out at dinner and she had no brothers or sisters. This was one of the few things that she and David had in common.

David stared at her. She was really short and very pretty. "Come here." He held his arms out and she came and sat in his lap. He put his big arms around her and she played with his big hands, covering her little ones with them.

"Maybe there's some way to make us a stronger couple." Amanda put her cheek next to David's. She smelled of a perfume that David couldn't name, something with jasmine. He breathed it in. He looked at his hairy wrist against her ribs.

"I don't know—don't you think we're already pretty strong?" David sighed.

"We could be stronger, like if we swore undying love to each other."

"We've already done that. Look, you're making me feel all unbalanced and uneven, like I did during the one and only time I did mushrooms and had to spend the whole night at Jonathan's house watching women's tennis. Really, we're going to be fine."

"*I just want to really believe in our love,*" Amanda whispered into David's neck.

"I don't know what I can do to make it any more real." David furrowed his brow.

"I know!" Amanda leaped up quickly, throwing on a white silk bathrobe. "Let's get engaged."

David stood too, and stared at Amanda. She was breathing quickly and her eyes were round. She was so much shorter than him that she often looked straight up at him, and sometimes her round face looked like a plate.

"Um, doesn't that seem a little intense?"

"Look, I don't want to ever cheat on you again and this'll keep my guard up—because it'll be like, illegal."

"Well, okay. We'll get engaged if you really want to. But right now I've got to get home and do my trig homework." David bent over and slipped his sneakers back on, which he'd kicked off only a few minutes earlier.

"So you're going to ask me to marry you, right? And then it'll be a pact between us—but of course we don't actually have to get married till we're like, twenty-five," Amanda said while they walked to her front door.

"I guess that's okay. I'll see you tomorrow night."

"Definitely," Amanda said. They kissed good-bye, which involved Amanda reaching up to pull David down to a kissable height. It started out as just a peck, but the elevator was taking a long time, so they started

51

making out pretty seriously against the wall. As David slipped his big hand inside Amanda's robe, he wondered whether or not it was a good thing that Amanda thought they needed to get legally married—engaged, whatever—just so they wouldn't cheat on each other again. This dimly reminded him of some psychological thing his father had once taught him about people who had a hard time controlling themselves, but with Amanda kissing his ear, he definitely couldn't remember what it was.

## a monday at school that I so cannot take
## seriously

Arno and I stood in front of a table piled high with neon-colored polo shirts on the second floor of the Ralph Lauren store and mansion on Madison. Gissing Academy let upperclassmen out for lunch and I'd convinced Arno to come with me to buy something for the trip with my dad, since he'd said I should, and Arno had nothing better to do.

We have a funny problem, Arno and I. We're the only people we really get along with at Gissing. I mean, we have plenty of buddies, but we don't take them that seriously. Then the weird part is, of our real friends, we're close, but we're not each other's favorites. I'm better friends with Patch, and then David, and then Mickey, than I am with Arno. And Arno's better friends with Mickey, and then Patch, and then David, who he's had some trouble with over Amanda, which had made them kind of intense with each other. But the weird part is, because we go to school together, Arno and I hang out pretty much constantly. So we're more like brothers than friends—not that that's a bad thing. And now that I'd invited him to the Caribbean instead of my other guys, it was like we were both questioning if we were actually closer than either one of us thought.

"Do you really think you can pull off hot pink?" Arno asked. He yawned. We had woken up at his house, made ourselves a big breakfast, and then been late to school. We'd muddled through morning classes and now we just had to get through an afternoon full of science, history electives, and Latin, and then we were out.

"Nah." I wandered toward a tan jacket made of windbreaker material. It had lots of pockets all over it and cost four hundred ninety-five dollars. There was a saleslady called Mary who was hovering around us. She was about my mom's age.

"Do you think it works?" she asked. Mary took me kind of seriously. I'd been buying clothes from her since I was ten.

"I'm not sure," I said. What the hell does someone need to wear to hike in the waterfalls in Venezuela, anyway? I pulled out my cell phone and held down the number 4, which speed-dialed Mickey.

He picked up on the third ring and said, "One sec."

I could hear his teacher yelling at him that no cell phones were allowed in class. After a moment it got quieter and I assumed Mickey was going into the hallway to talk, which is what he always did when I called him during the day at school. Of course talking on cell phones at school wasn't allowed, but Mickey has this way of repelling rules or something. Like he's got a magnetic force, and no matter how much someone yells at him or gives him detention, it never really pans out.

"Dude, I'm in Ralph Lauren and I need your advice on this windbreaker. I like it, but more importantly, I need to know if this is the kind of thing you wear when you're hiking or doing something else outside that's like that."

"Where are *you* going hiking?" He said this like it was the craziest idea he'd ever heard.

"Well, there's some shit happening with me, and I can't really go into it all, but the most important thing for you to know at this moment is that my dad is getting remarried and he asked me to go on the honeymoon with him and his new wife and her son, who is named Serge and apparently likes to hike and do stuff like that, and no way am I going to be showed up by some foreign kid who likes adventure shit."

"Whoa, buddy," Mickey said. "First of all, that's sort of rough about your dad and I'm sorry. Secondly, where is this hiking happening, and third, can I come? I can help you with the outdoorsy stuff."

I knew that if this was anyone but Mickey, I'd think he was being a little forward, but the whole candid thing was part of what made him so awesome. And at that moment, I was totally sure he was the guy that I wanted with me to confront my dad and Serge and PISS and whatever weird bugs or other animals might be out in nature. I looked around for Arno and caught a glimpse of him in front of the antique watch counter, flirting with a blond girl in a black suit. She was rubbing perfume into his pulse points.

"All through the Caribbean on this huge sailboat, and yeah, I'd really like you to come with me. It's just—"

"Awesome. Better head back in before I get detention for a week."

"Mickey, there's one other thing . . ." But he'd already clicked off. I handed my American Express card to Mary and told her I'd take the jacket with all the pockets. I went over to Arno while she rang it up.

"Smell this," he said.

"Yeah, you smell good, like a girl who just took a bath."

"That's right. Now while I'm at school and bored this afternoon, I'll be able to smell girls because I smell like one! Smart, huh?"

"Yeah, brilliant." The saleswoman smiled and gave Arno her card. Then Mary came back and handed me my card and a shiny blue RL bag, and we walked back to school. It was incredibly bright out, and not too cold. Normally Arno would have spent a walk like that making fun of me for the girls I'm currently not hanging around with, like Fernanda, who goes to Barnard and said she was too mature for me, and Patch's little sister, Flan, who is way too young but weirdly cool, and Liza Komansky (but we never talk about her since Arno fooled around with her a month or so ago), but instead he just kept smelling himself and smiling.

We were near school and we began to say our

*what's ups* to guys as they passed. Among the many things that are a drag about going to an all-boys school is that you have to say "what's up" constantly. It's exhausting.

"What's up," Arno muttered. "Liesel's cousin is having a bunch of people to his apartment tonight. I'm one of the hosts, so you have to come. This is a new group. You'll like them . . ."

"What's up," I said to some doped-out-looking senior.

"What's up," Arno said to some guy in his English class.

"If we're going to go out tonight," I said, "I need to go home and get some clothes this afternoon."

"Sounds good. What's up, babydoll?" But Arno had said it to Mrs. Nathanson, our English teacher, and that made us both laugh.

## after-school milk and cookies with mickey and philippa

"I'm just saying what I heard," Philippa said to Mickey.

"Well, what you heard is bullshit." Mickey covered a tumbler with a paper towel and slammed it down on his kitchen counter. The contents sizzled and he shot it back, his eyes watering.

"Nice one," Philippa said. "Now do me."

Monday afternoon, and they were over at Mickey's house doing their Monday afternoon ritual, which was tequila slammers and TiVo'd gossip shows from the Style network that Philippa watched obsessively. She was very into gossip.

"I talked to Jonathan today. Yeah, his dad is getting remarried, but it doesn't sound like he's in any kind of financial trouble. He invited me to go on a trip with them on some gi-normous sailboat through the Caribbean."

Even though it was November, Mickey was in blue

canvas shorts, flip-flops, and a white leather jacket. He went over to the stereo and turned on the new Yeah Yeah Yeahs CD.

Philippa turned off the TV.

"Listen," she said. "I don't like my dad any more than you do yours. But that doesn't make him a liar. He said he hopes Jonathan's dad isn't spending too much on the wedding, because everyone is about to sue the living daylights out of him for stealing lots of people's money."

"Yeah, bullshit."

Philippa smiled at Mickey, who was crouched on the counter like a big monkey, messing around with the stereo. Mickey was ignoring Philippa, which was odd, since she was wearing only a white Marc Jacobs blouse and her underwear. They'd been fooling around in the living room, on the gigantic horseshoe-shaped couch Mickey's dad had built there. The thing was twenty feet long and made of ultrathick purple velvet.

"Make me a slammer," Philippa said. Mickey kissed the top of her forehead. Then, still crouched on the counter, he set her up with a slammer. But he wouldn't look her in the eye.

"You're sensitive about Jonathan."

"Come on, baby. All this rumor stuff is crazy—his dad is obviously still rich and even if he wasn't, what the hell does it matter to us?"

"It's not a rumor. It's just what my dad said."
Philippa shrugged. "When are your parents getting
home?"

"What you described is a rumor," Mickey said.
"They're here, I think."

"Your parents?!"

Mickey raised the mix of half-tequila-half-ginger-ale
over his head.

"Mickey?"

"Hi, Mom."

Philippa scooted around the kitchen island, but
Lucy Pardo, Mickey's mom, still caught an eyeful of
Philippa's barely covered behind.

"I thought we discussed that tequila slammers are
for special occasions," Lucy Pardo said.

"Yeah," Mickey said. "It's Monday and next week is
Thanksgiving. That's special."

"Hi, Mrs. Pardo."

"Go find your jeans, sweetie."

"Okay," Philippa said weakly. She skipped into the
living room to find her jeans and her shoes.

"Your father will be in Montauk this week, but I'm
staying here. Now *deja de emborracharte en las tardes!*"
*Stop drinking in the afternoons!*

"Sorry, Mom."

Mickey hopped down from the counter. The slammer he'd been holding bubbled over.

"But don't let this go to waste. You have it." Mickey handed the shot to his mother. She shot it. After wiping her mouth, she looked for Philippa, who was half hidden behind a Yoshi screen in the living room.

"You two behave yourselves. I'm serious. No more drinking and partying in this house on school days." Then she walked out of the room.

"Wow," Philippa said. "My dad's right. Your mom really is from another planet."

"Your dad should keep his nose out of other people's business!"

"He also said you had a temper that I'm just not seeing and that you're too wild for me and I should deal with that."

"STOP IT!" Mickey yelled. Then he dropped to his knees in front of Philippa and clasped his hands together. "Please never listen to your dad again. Can you do that for me? And can you let all this gossip go? You're getting way, way, too into it."

"I don't know." Philippa shook her head and fished a piece of dark chocolate out of a bowl on the counter. She chewed and looked away from Mickey, who was still on his knees, and then she said, "I get grounded so much because of hanging out with you, I kind of have to depend on hearing everything second-hand from whoever was actually there. It's either that, or I hear stuff from my parents."

"Well, maybe you and me shouldn't get into so much trouble anymore, then."

"Do you think that's even possible?" Philippa licked her fingers.

"I don't know," Mickey said. "Let's try."

### the tent that's pitched in my living room

"Hello!" I yelled. The door to my apartment was open when Richard, the old elevator man, let me out in my hallway. He slammed the elevator door shut behind me.

All the furniture in my apartment had been moved to some undisclosed location, so now the home I grew up in was nearly empty. In the middle of the dining room was what looked like a great jumble of the stuff of ours that was too small to bother moving, all hidden under a big white sheet.

I sighed and went down the hall toward my room. To my left, in the living room, there was a tent. A green tent.

"Hello!"

"Yeaagh!" I kind of jumped against the wall. Behind me, there was a tall, thin guy with shaggy brown hair. He was wearing painter's overalls and no shirt or shoes. He held a pair of my mother's chandelier earrings.

"Found these in an egg cup in the fridge. Seems to me all has not been at ease here."

"Huh?"

"I'm Billy Shanlon. We met when you were into sculpting shoes out of sand, just a few years ago. I assume you're Jonathan. That right?"

"That's right."

"Well, I'm your painter."

We stood there. His face was contorted in a jack-o'-lantern grin and his hair hung around his head like tufts of brown cotton. He was at least half a foot taller than me, and I'm not short.

Around us the floors were covered in swirls of white canvas and old sheets, so what was once my wonderfully familiar apartment had become pretty much unrecognizable. The smell of paint was everywhere, too, but it didn't look as if Billy Shanlon had begun to apply any of it to the walls.

"Did you touch my clothes?" I asked.

"Burned 'em."

"Ha." I immediately turned and ran down the hall toward my room. He was right behind me, and I could feel him laughing.

"So you're a fancy boy?"

"The hell I am. Where are you from, anyway, Ireland?"

"Long Island, actually. Riverhead."

This was a place I knew only from seeing road signs when I rode the Jitney to the Hamptons to visit my friends. I got into my room and, sadly enough, everything that hadn't been dragged out and stuffed on a truck somewhere was in a great heap with a sheet over it.

"Feels unsettling, doesn't it?" Billy Shanlon nodded to himself and scratched his stubbly chin.

I opened my closet. Empty. *Shit.*

"I need a sweater," I said.

He rummaged around for a moment underneath the sheet and came up with a stack of sweaters, mostly dark blue or black cashmere.

"Here." He handed me my sweaters and I stood there, holding them.

Billy leaned against my window, which was open. Cold air blew in, but he seemed totally unconcerned. He pulled out an American Spirit and lit it. He smoked and smiled at me in this weird, lazy way.

"Don't you think you should get started?" I asked. "I thought you were here to paint the apartment."

66

"I am. But I'm waiting for inspiration. In the meantime, if you want to just come by and hang out and talk, that's cool."

"I'll stop by when I need a shirt," I said.

## arno's new girlfriend's cousin throws a little get-together

"I'll admit," Arno said, "this is not my regular beat."

Arno stood with Jonathan and David on Central Park West and Sixty-second Street, looking up at a glistening white Art Deco building. They were on the park side of the street. The only light came from yellow street lamps, which made the street feel very retro and otherworldly and nothing like downtown. Up on the eighth floor, they could see kids moving back and forth in silhouette.

"She's meeting you in there, right?" David asked.

"I hope so," Arno said.

"I'm psyched for this party, actually," David said. "A lot of Potterton kids live up here. Most of them, actually, if you think about it. And I barely ever talk to any of them."

"Well, good," Arno agreed.

"Speaking of new people," Jonathan turned to David, "I haven't told you that my dad's getting remarried and I'm getting a stepbrother."

"Yeah, my dad said your mom said some stuff was going on with your family. That's kind of weird, huh?" David said. "You all right with all that?"

"It's cool, I guess," Jonathan said.

"It's more than cool," Arno interjected. "His dad is marrying some unbelievably rich woman named PISS who is taking us sailing through the Caribbean on a three-hundred-foot yacht!"

"Yeah?" David looked hopeful.

"Yeah," Jonathan said, but then he wrinkled his nose and started looking flustered. "But 'we' is actually . . ." he trailed off. "C'mon, let's just go up."

The three of them went across the street. They'd called Patch earlier, but he wasn't around. And Mickey and Philippa had said they were staying home to study, which everyone agreed was a total lie.

"You think Liesel will talk with us this time, before you and her go somewhere and make out?" Jonathan asked in the elevator.

"Hard to say." Arno smiled. He didn't bother to pretend as if he knew what Liesel would do. He still felt like he hardly knew her—and he was beginning to realize that was part of what made her so exciting. Arno sniffed the air. "You smell like paint," he said.

"So what? You still smell like a girl."

When they walked in, the birthday party was in full swing.

"Awww-no!" a girl yelled.

"Ready, set, go," Arno said as Liesel enveloped him in a nutcracker hug. He hugged her back. She picked him up. He picked her up.

"We're going to have to pry them off the ceiling," Jonathan said to David.

"These are your awesome friends," Liesel said.

She kissed them both on the cheek three times while Arno watched. She stood there in a gold cropped V-neck T-shirt and a black skirt that was about nine inches long. Arno smiled. He thought, *maybe she's charming—maybe I'm really into how brash she is*. But he felt like he was looking at her through blurry eyes—he couldn't be sure about anything about her. He followed Liesel into the kitchen, which was old-fashioned and huge, with a maid's room and a pantry. The surfaces of antique cabinets were reflected in the aluminum faces of twenty-first-century appliances.

"Whose house is this, anyway?"

"Alan Ebershoff's," Liesel said. "He's my cousin. You should call him Froggy." She yanked over a heavyset boy with long blond hair that covered his eyes. He was wearing baggy red corduroys, no shoes, and a blue turtleneck.

"You guys want drinks?" Ebershoff had a voice like a bullfrog.

"Sure we do," Arno said.

In the middle of the white marble counter was a gigantic piece of dry ice that was giving off puffs of smoke. Several kids stood around watching it, as if the ice were going to start to talk or move. There was a carved-out area in the center of the dry ice that held several bottles of vodka.

"Here ya go," the bullfrog croaked. Arno accepted a glass of vodka, lemon, and ice.

"Thanks, man."

Jonathan and David got drinks and quickly went into the living room. Arno watched them go.

"I've been thinking about you," Liesel said, pressing into Arno's back. He leaned against her and thought she smelled of alcohol and a different perfume than he'd had on earlier, perhaps Chanel No. 9, which Arno realized he recognized because his mother wore it. *Gross.* He tried to forget the connection.

"Let's get you into a bedroom," Liesel said.

"Um, good idea."

They took their drinks and disappeared down a hallway. Arno watched her small, twitchy butt as she walked. He slowed down, but only because he wasn't smiling and smirking the way he usually did before hooking up, and he couldn't understand why.

"*Hurry up!*" Liesel yelled. Several other guys jumped to attention when she yelled, but she was only looking at Arno. So he got his face in order, tried to close his nose, and hurried.

"And awaaa-y they go," I said.

"*I feel like if we said hello to her again, she wouldn't know our names,*" David whispered.

"Yeah. We're just the awesome friends. She's not into details."

We watched Arno and Liesel disappear down a dimly lit hall and close a door behind them.

"If anyone's going to take over this kid's parents' bedroom, it should be them," I said.

"She could break Arno in half," David said as we wandered into the living room. His phone buzzed, and he looked at the screen.

"Mickey?" I asked.

He shook his head, glanced out the window. Alan Ebershoff came in and put on some Jimi Hendrix, really loud. Some guys stood in a circle, and then out came the Hacky Sack.

"Patch?" I asked. Still no. David typed something back.

"Risa Subkoff," David said.

"Who?"

"I don't feel terrific about this." David was IMing his location to Risa Subkoff. I looked over his shoulder.

"Don't tell me you have a thing with this Risa Subkoff."

"Maybe I do."

"What's your name again? Do you mind if I call you Arno?"

"Come on," David said. "Don't pigeonhole me. I know I'm not Arno, but maybe I need to kick it with two different girls for a while."

"Nah. You shouldn't even *say* kick it." *David was juggling two girls*? He might as well have told me he was getting paid to have sex with them, which was about as believable.

But then David's screen said *be right there* and David smiled. He said, "She plays basketball for Trinity. We saw each other play this afternoon and then we talked and then . . ." He smiled. "I'm going to the bathroom and clean myself up before she gets here."

"At least give me an explanation," I said, and I downed a lot of my drink. A sweet girl called Madison, whom I knew from my days at Camp

Meadowlark, filled my glass with more cold vodka.

"Well, I was at Amanda's yesterday and she told me she wants to be engaged, which of course is insane, but she says we need to do it so we won't cheat on each other again."

"So when she said that, you knew she must be cheating on you, so you figured you'd cheat on her again too?"

"Precisely." David smiled and raised his glass in a toast to me. "I talked about it with my dad for a minute, without naming names. He said even if she hasn't already, she's going to."

"But you love her."

"Yeah, but we have problems, and this girl Risa, she's really nice to me and we actually have stuff in common, which obviously Amanda and I don't."

"Because you're basically interested in basketball and psychology. And you don't like to deal with that second part of you, so a basketball-playing girl is like a dream come true."

"Right again." David raised his thick eyebrows and padded off. He turned around for a second when he got to the hallway, though, and said, "Hey, let's talk more about your dad later, okay?"

I nodded a nod that said *yeah, thanks*, but then I figured it was now or never. I had to tell him.

"Hey, David?" I walked across the room to get closer to him.

"Yeah?"

"The thing is . . . I'm not exactly sure how to say this, but I can only take one friend on this trip. So, you know . . ." I trailed off.

But David smiled. "Damn. I'm sure Arno's gonna be bummed, but that's really cool of you to want me to be there, man. We're going to have such a great time!"

He turned back toward the bathroom, and I felt my whole body sag. That certainly hadn't gone as planned.

Some kids watched him walk off and whispered to each other. Even though to me—to us— he was David the Mope, to other people he was one of the best basketball players in the private school leagues, and certainly the star of Potterton's team. But that didn't fool me into thinking he was cool, even though he was a great friend. I thought all his parents' psychobabble had worn off on him in a good way.

So now I'd managed to invite Arno, Mickey, and David all on a trip where I could only take one of them, and worse, David thought he was The One. It occurred to me then that maybe this whole guilt over my dad being a criminal thing was subconsciously making me bribe my friends, kind of like when my parents got divorced and my Christmas presents suddenly got a whole lot better. I thought about this as I took a sip of my drink, which was no longer cold and simply tasted like extremely potent alcohol.

Suddenly, a whole group of girls came into the living room. I could tell instantly that they were it—the enviable group that all these uptown kids talked about. Conversations quieted while they settled in. It was easy to see that they knew everyone was watching them.

I finished my drink while I, too, watched them, and the dregs of that second glass of warm vodka hit my belly like an elbow-jam on the subway. I lurched and took a seat on one end of a black leather couch. The place was pretty modern looking, with a huge thing on the floor that was more of a mat than a rug and looked like an oil slick, and a lot of black and chrome furniture placed at odd angles throughout the living room.

That girl Madison walked through with one of the smoking icy bottles of Absolut Peppar, and I held up my glass.

"Careful." She smiled.

I sipped. It was like sipping water and then having someone snap a wet towel against your lips. I hit it again. *Ow.*

"If you're going to play old stuff, play The Band," a voice said.

"Whatever you say, Ruth." I watched Froggy hop away to a hidden place where the stereo must've been.

I looked up.

There was a girl attached to the voice. She had long honey-colored hair, and she was wearing a short purple skirt. In the black and silvery light of that living room, she had a golden yellow color all around her.

"*The girl in the long gray coat,*" I whispered.

Froggy put on "Up on Cripple Creek" and she started to dance. Her other friends danced too. They didn't seem to be drinking. I pushed my glass aside, but I didn't feel like I could hop up and dance. How could I get to her?

That's when she threw herself down next to me and smiled.

"I know who you are," she said.

"Yeah, I've seen you before, too."

"You're best friends with Arno Wildenburger. Have you seen him tonight?"

I shook my head. *Not Arno*. Once girls got Arno on the brain, it was like a disease in a horror movie. They turned into screaming monsters and could not be changed back until he hooked up with them and blew them off.

She laughed. A tinkly tender noise that made me think that in order to hear it again, I'd do a lot. I'd do anything. And it was funny, because her laugh was a good contrast to her voice, which was sort of low and nasal—if a voice can be both those things at the same time.

"I don't *want* him. I just want to check in with Liesel."

"You're her friend?"

"We go to Nightingale together. We have one of those friendships where we're close, but— whatever, I've known her forever."

"That's how I am with Arno!" Some of her friends looked over and smiled. I'd been loud. I was drunk.

"Where are you from?" I asked. "Tell me everything about you. But first—do you have a cold?"

That's when David walked up with someone

almost as tall as him.

"This is Risa," David said. I looked up and David had a female twin: a big dark-haired girl who was clearly destined for the UConn Huskies and the WNBA.

"Hey." She held out her hand. I took it and it was like shaking with David.

"I'm Ruth," the girl sitting next to me said. I realized that, even though we'd been basically saying nothing, she and I had managed to sort of snuggle up to each other. She was warm. I had my hand slipped around her waist, and slowly we extracted ourselves from each other. How had that happened?

"This is a good party," I said. Ruth giggled.

We heard a whoop from the kitchen. All of us wandered in there, since everyone in the living room was swaying to "The Night They Drove Old Dixie Down" and laughing.

In the kitchen, the lights were off and Froggy was attacking the dry ice with a two-foot-long cleaver that his parents probably used to hack Thanksgiving turkeys to pieces. Bits of dry ice were skittering around on the tile floor and everyone was egging Froggy on while protecting their eyes. It was only a matter of time before the cleaver connected with the Grey Goose bottles in the middle of the ice, and then there'd be a real mess.

"Why is he doing that?" Ruth asked. Her eyes were a little watery around the edges, and every time I looked at her, she was smiling. That made me smile too, that and her crazy voice.

"Because it's his house and no one can make him stop."

I realized I was holding Ruth's hand. We edged into a pantry.

"Can we spend some time together some-time?" I asked.

"Yes. Yes, let's find each other."

"Let's definitely do that."

I reached to kiss her and there was an unbe-lievably loud crash that shook the whole pantry. Cans of overpriced vegetables from France rained from the shelves.

"The dry ice didn't do that," I said, covering our heads.

There was another crash, and then several smaller ones. Then quiet. We peeked out and saw Froggy drop the cleaver. Then he flipped the overhead lights on. The ice was still intact.

"Hmm," Ruth said. We crept through the

kitchen into the living room. Someone had turned off the music.

It was as quiet as it would've been if Froggy's parents had walked in. Then we heard muffled laughter and some whooping noises coming from another part of the apartment. Froggy took off running down the hall.

"Uh oh." David turned to me. I nodded. We waited and then there was the sound of Froggy screaming.

"My parents' bed!" The Frog screamed as he came running back to us. "They crashed it through the floor!"

He stood in the middle of the living room, swinging what appeared to be a large piece of his parents' bed that looked like an unfinished section of an aluminum baseball bat.

Behind him, Arno came out of the hallway. He was pulling up his pants. Liesel was wearing Arno's jacket, a bra, panties, and no skirt. Her high heels were still on, though.

"Cool it, Alan," Liesel said. "We were only playing."

"Everybody out!"

Arno zipped up his pants. He grabbed a glass that was sitting on an end table and took a sip.

"Dude, that thing was so rickety—"

"Out!"

"Ruth," Liesel screamed over Froggy's voice. "You made it!"

Liesel came over and the two of them hugged hello and everyone watched since Leisel was pretty much naked.

"Out!" Froggy screamed again.

"Froggy's got a temper and he did ride," some kid sang out. We scrambled around and figured out where the stairs were, since The Frog clearly didn't want us waiting for the elevator, and then we streamed out of there like mice escaping a sinking ship.

"We've got to get across town." Liesel sounded like she could only hang out on the Upper West Side for so many hours before she started to melt. "We'll see you boys very soon."

Ruth hugged me and kissed me on the cheek.

It took about one second for a cab to stop for the two girls, probably because Liesel was still wearing next to nothing.

"Call me," Ruth said. "Get Arno to get my number from Liesel. Call me tomorrow."

"I will."

And they were gone.

"Hey," Arno said. "That girl liked you."

I looked up at the sky. Sure enough, I could see one star. That's how you know it's a good night in New York City, when you can see just one big star.

## david thinks he lives alone

"I want you," David said simply, to Risa. He'd grabbed a cab from the party, rather than hanging around to see what happened. They slipped into the lobby of his building. The night doorman, Jordy, was fast asleep. They got into the old elevator.

"You're sure about this?" Risa said.

"Why wouldn't I be?" David asked. He'd turned his phone off so he wouldn't get calls from Amanda and Jonathan. He knew he was still getting the hang of behaving badly, but he was determined to get there, to the bad place where he thought Arno lived. He told himself that ever since Amanda had cheated on him with Arno, he'd been waiting for what he hoped was about to happen.

"It's your parents' house. Do they mind you bringing girls home in the middle of the night?"

"What? Oh yeah. No. They live like half a block down from me if you think about distance inside apartments that way, and they always go to sleep early. And

I've been—I want you to come upstairs with me."

"Do you do this a lot?"

"No way," David said. "Only when I feel really into someone, like the way I feel about you."

"That's sweet. Because I know you have one of those over-the-top relationships with Amanda Harrison Deutschmann . . ." Risa's voice had a bit of bass to it, a thrumming noise that reverberated in the elevator. They were up against one wall, fooling around, like they'd been doing in the cab.

". . . and I wouldn't want to ruin what you and her—"

"No more words," David said, and put a fingertip over Risa's lips. She closed her eyes and kissed it. They were both wearing gigantic basketball sneakers that squeaked on the elevator floor. When the doors opened they lurched out to the hallway. David carefully took out his keys. He thought of Amanda, how much he loved her, the tiny cuteness of her, the amazing fall they'd had together. He'd been flirting with Risa after games for only a couple weeks and he had no idea why he was so compelled to cheat—except that now this crazy getting-engaged thing had combined with the fact that they were always breaking up, and that Amanda said he didn't have enough class for her, and that she was always analyzing him like his parents did, and . . . He eased the door open.

"We're in," he said. Risa giggled. Her thick black hair brushed his face as they went into the hallway. David had her around the waist. He thought, *I hardly know this girl.*

"Which way to your bedroom?" she whispered.

"Hold my hand."

"David?"

A light went on in the living room to David's right, and there was his father, wearing an ancient red wool bathrobe and cracked leather slippers.

"Dad?" David's voice was strangled.

"I had something important . . ." Sam Grobart's voice trailed off. He'd been fast asleep. "I had to see you as soon as possible. Who is this?"

"Just a girl from, um, a party. She came over to borrow something."

Sam Grobart looked at the grandfather clock. It was two-thirty in the morning.

"You have something she can't get through the night without? Where's Amanda?" David's father asked.

"I think I better go," Risa said.

"*He's talking in his sleep*," David whispered quickly. "*He'll go away in a minute.*"

His father opened his mouth, and then glared suddenly. "Take this girl down to the lobby and get her a cab."

"I'll do it myself." Risa turned around and went back down the corridor and out the front door.

"Risa, wait."

"Don't follow her," Mr. Grobart said as the door of the apartment slammed shut. "If she likes you, she'll call you tomorrow and you can both blame your old man. And in the meantime, you can break up with your girlfriend. Hmm? Anyway, come sit down with me."

"Now?" David asked.

"You were planning on staying up late and talking meaningfully with her, weren't you? Why not with me?"

Sam Grobart raised the thick eyebrow that ran in a straight line over both his eyes and stared at his son. They went into the living room, where books covered every surface. In the few spots not covered with books, there were magazines and stacks of papers. Sam Grobart eased himself back into his black leather chair. He pointed to a spot on the couch across from him, and David sat down. David couldn't believe it. Within minutes he'd gone from potentially having something really intense happen in his bedroom with a girl he didn't know very well to the all-consuming familiarity of his living room and a forced conversation with his dad. He tried a yawn, but his dad wasn't biting.

"What I have to say is about your friend Jonathan."

"What about him? I was just with him."

"Starting now, he's going to go through a very tough time."

"Yeah, he told me that his dad is getting remarried. That's rough, I get it."

"Yes, that's part of it. But there's more. I should start from the beginning."

"Dad, it's kind of late . . ."

"Your mother and I went to Brown with Jonathan's father, along with a number of our other friends. He was a very sweet man whom none of us expected to amount to much, and when we moved back to the city after college—"

Sam Grobart stopped. David's eyes had drooped.

"Long story short?" Sam asked.

"Please."

"His father was doing accounting for all our families. This was back in the eighties, when monkeys and children were making fortunes. So he began to invest for us, and for the Wildenburgers, and the Pardos, and the Floods, among others. But things went bad with his marriage, as you know. He fled to London. No one saw him after that. And now he's getting married again."

"Right, I already know this."

"You know I feel that if something concerns you, you should know about it, so I'm going to tell you some things I learned from Jonathan's mother. But I do think that what I'm about to tell you shouldn't be shared just yet. Okay?"

"I don't get it. What are you trying to tell me?"

"Howard—Jonathan's father—he's a thief. Ah, it feels good to say that. He stole a few hundred thousand dollars from us. Lord knows what he took from our richer friends. Anyway, the reason this concerns you is that I want you to be there for Jonathan for the next few weeks. Clearly his mother can't be counted on to take care of him."

"Why not?"

"Because she left town."

"Oh, right."

There was quiet in the living room for a moment, only punctuated with the ticking of a variety of clocks, all set incorrectly.

"There's more to the story, but—who was that girl?"

"I'm beat, Dad," David said. "I better hit the sack."

"Oh, me too. I've got to stop falling asleep when I'm with patients. They're starting to resent me for it."

"At least you're not leaving them bankrupt."

"Some would disagree." Sam Grobart cackled to himself as he got up and shuffled down the dark corridor to the bedroom he shared with his wife. David stood in the living room, looking at the peeling paint and stacks and stacks of books. He couldn't believe it.

Jonathan was the son of a swindler. Then again, everyone said Arno's dad was a bit of a con man. And Mickey's dad charged outrageous amounts for the cars he destroyed and sold as art. And everybody said Patch's dad had never put in an honest day's work in his life. And then David remembered: Risa. *Damn!*

"She was amazing," I said to Arno, who was not awake yet.

Okay, first things first: my physical shape was bad. I smelled like old spilled beer. But damn! She was so beautiful. And the smell of whatever that retro stuff she wore. Patchouli? Mmm. I lay there and I was *happy*. I'd smiled at a girl on the street, and then just weeks later she was kissing me on the cheek. This was a major, major crush.

I hadn't totally had one on Fernanda, the Barneys girl, 'cause that would have been too much like falling in love with your addiction (I am addicted to shoes—my mother has forced me to admit this). And the thing with Flan was more like sweetness and avoidance. But *this*. I rubbed my knees together, and then I felt that I was still wearing socks. And then I realized that in addition to the socks, I still had on pants and my shirt.

"Hey, dude," Arno said. "It's Tuesday."

And everything crashed together—like when I was sock-skating down the hall in my house when I was five and my mom swung open her bedroom door and the brass doorknob connected with my forehead and floored me. My house was being painted by a complete weirdo, my dad was some kind of thief, I'd invited three of my four best friends on a trip when only one was allowed to come, and I suddenly had no doubt that my guys were about to start figuring it all out.

"Oh man," I groaned.

"She was a cutie. Most definitely," Arno said. So I knew that he'd misunderstood my groan and thought I was happy, which was definitely how I'd been all last night. Arno's phone beeped; he picked it up, looked at it briefly, and then tossed the phone over to me.

"It's your girl's information, from Liesel."

I forwarded the message to my phone.

"I can't wait to talk to her."

"I'll bet," Arno said. "You two were all over each other."

I scrambled around and tried to sit up in the bed. Wait, there was no bed. I looked up. Arno was in a bed. I was lying on the floor under a bright orange blanket that had been made by some Italian artist.

I remembered her face. She'd been so sweet. *Ruth.*

"Let's go over to Florent and get some breakfast." Arno stood up and stretched.

"You sure you don't want to hang around here? And then later, maybe go to school?"

"Nah," Arno said. "Lately I get miserable being anywhere near my parents. But yeah, we could go to school. Let's just go to Florent for some eggs first."

He found some loafers and put them on. And then I remembered what was going on with his parents.

"You're right, let's get out of here." I struggled to stand.

## lovers quarrel over the shape of clouds
## in the sky

Mickey and Philippa were hanging around Mickey's house on Tuesday night, trying not to get into trouble again. Mickey had a huge desire to go out and do something insane, but being totally in love with Philippa was kind of squelching that feeling.

"You have a way of making me want to sit home and drink milk," he said.

"That's romantic," Philippa said, and she sounded like she kind of meant it. "It's the new, clean us—and if we stay this way, maybe my parents will even start being nice to you."

"Wow," Mickey said. And then they locked eyes and started to fool around very intensely because that was the only relatively harmless thing they could think of to do—and since they'd been hanging out at home alone, they'd been doing it constantly.

They were in the Pardo living room, which was massive and blanketed in art, and which resembled the hall of a medieval castle. They were sprawled out on the huge purple couch and took breaks from kissing to sip beer from shiny cans of Sapporo. Mickey was in billowy black shorts and an I ❤ KAREN O T-shirt. Over the last couple of days he'd rediscovered shorts and remembered how much he liked them.

"Have you talked to anybody today?"

"Only at school." Philippa rubbed her eyes. She had allergies and the rugs in the Pardo house all came from exotic animals.

"Did you hear anything about Liesel's party?" Mickey asked.

"Just that we missed a good time."

To Mickey, it sounded a little like Philippa wished she'd been there. They were quiet. She handed him the beer. He sipped it, and smiled at her.

He could feel the need to go out and break stuff rumbling in his chest. He knew that this just wasn't his nature, that no matter how much he loved Philippa, he couldn't sit at home and study and fool around much longer. Then his cell rang and he fumbled around on the floor to get it. Unlike, say, Jonathan, who had the latest Motorola with all the extras, Mickey was content with an old phone of his dad's that was about the size of a softball, and that he had to punch a few times after it rang to get a connection. It was David.

"I heard that Ebershoff kid attacked you with a meat cleaver last night," Mickey said.

"Close," David said. "But we got out of there. Where were you?"

"Same place I am now. Behaving myself, with my girl."

"Gawd," David said. "Listen, something weird is happening with Jonathan."

"Yeah, his dad's getting married, right?" Mickey was stroking Philippa's hair. So long and brown. He kissed her cheek. In the background, the Beatles' *Abbey Road* played softly.

"That's part of it. What else do you know?"

"Well, he called because he wanted to know what clothes to buy for hiking or hang gliding." Mickey looked at Philippa, who was picking at her cuticle. "I'm going with him on some sailing trip to the jungle or something."

"You are?" David asked. "But I am, too."

Philippa went to change the music. She was wearing a long red dress, and it flowed behind her. The room was so big that it took time to get to the wall with the stereo controls, and she seemed to glide, like a ghost. Mickey watched her.

"Great. I'm sure we all are. What's the problem?" Mickey frowned. If David was about to confirm the stuff Philippa had been saying the night before, then maybe the trip would be off after all.

"Well, Jonathan told me only one of us could come. And that it's me," David said.

Mickey could hear David breathing heavily into the phone.

"Oh. Well, that's kind of lame of him to invite me, too, then," Mickey said, and started picking at his cuticle, like Philippa.

"Yeah, and he invited Arno."

"Huh."

"But wait—there's this other thing that my dad said Jonathan's mom told him about his dad that's even worse—"

"Isn't your dad not supposed to talk about things he's learned from patients?" Mickey asked. He'd visited many therapists and counselors over the years, so he knew the rules.

"Yeah," David said. "I guess he feels like he's beyond that rule. But forget it, I think."

"I already have and he's not."

"Whatever, Mickey, the point is I'm telling you this thing about Jonathan, but now I'm actually kind of wondering why Jonathan is lying to all of us, or playing favorites, or whatever he's doing." David paused. "I think he feels guilty about some stuff." David could hear that he was channeling his dad. He shuddered.

"What kind of stuff?"

"Um, I don't know. Nothing." As annoyed as David was at Jonathan for being sketchy about the whole sailing-trip-thing and whom he had invited, he couldn't bring himself to tell Mickey about Jonathan's dad being a thief. That just seemed too huge.

"Well, let's not say anything to him if he doesn't say anything to us," Mickey said. "We'll see how long it takes for him to straighten this out." Mickey chuckled, but he was actually sort of bummed. He'd gotten excited about rafting in the Amazon, which he'd imagined doing on this trip. He wondered if David was wrong and maybe Jonathan did still plan on taking him, rather than David or Arno.

"Okay," David spoke quickly. "And I'll keep the other thing completely to myself. Deal?"

"Yeah, it's a deal," Mickey said with authority.

Philippa came back, having switched the music to a Dvořák symphony she loved because she'd played the piano when she was younger. The classical music started quietly and then began to thunder through the big room.

"Okay," Mickey said. "I'm holed up with Philippa but I'm sure I'll talk to you later."

Mickey got off the phone. He looked over to the

other side of the couch, where Philippa was stroking one of the family dogs, an old white greyhound called Blue. With her other hand, she covered her mouth and nose with a cloth napkin.

"What happened?" Philippa asked.

"Well," Mickey said. "It seems like Jonathan was only supposed to invite one friend on the wild sailing trip, but he invited me, David, and Arno, and maybe Patch, too, although I haven't talked to him in a while."

"Sorry, baby. I know you were excited about going," Philippa said. They lay there, quietly, in front of the ten-foot-high fireplace, surrounded by huge sculptures and paintings. In the distance, they could hear one of the housekeepers preparing hors d'oeuvres for the drinks hour that the Pardos had every day at six-thirty for whomever happened to be around the house, whether they were art dealers, collectors, or just Ricardo's staff of guys, who were always up for some eating.

"I think he'll still take me. I mean, I'd definitely be the most fun, and really, he'd probably fall of the edge of a cliff or something if I wasn't there to help him with all the outdoorsy stuff."

"Yeah," Philippa said. "But don't do anything too wild to prove that to him, okay?" Philippa was really good at reading Mickey's mind.

"I'll see what I can do." Mickey smiled mischievously at his beautiful, calm girlfriend and picked up a big log. He dropped it on the massive andirons his dad had made out of a park bench. "Got a match?"

Philippa flipped him some matches. He struck the match and threw it into the fireplace, and immediately the huge log was engulfed in flame. The Pardos soaked their logs in kerosene because they were too impatient to bother with kindling.

Philippa reached over and kissed Mickey, and he decided he could wait to prove to Jonathan that he was the most fun friend and thus definitely the guy to take on the trip. After all, he'd still be fun even after making out with Philippa some more, right? And before long they were rolling around together in front of the sputtering, flaming log.

**the joy of being somewhere i never am**

Ruth and I agreed to meet for tea at a little spot in Williamsburg, which is a neighborhood where I basically never go. For one thing, it's in Brooklyn, and for another, it's like visiting a college campus because there are so many hipsters streaming around. And honestly, twenty-five-year-old guys dressed up in whatever the guys from the Darkness wore the last time they played Bowery Ballroom can be a little trying. I mean, sometimes these hipsters just look old. And old hipsters are annoying.

But none of that mattered when I got off the L train on Bedford Avenue. The sun was setting and the sky was a sweet blue, etched with lines of white from airplane exhaust, and I was feeling mellow, as deeply mellow as I had since my mom left town. I shielded my eyes and looked around, trying to figure out which direction was south and how I was going to find the Bell Café, where

I was supposed to meet Ruth.

"Hey!"

And there she was. She grabbed my hand and we did this kind of awkward kiss thing, pretty much where we rubbed cheeks, but not entirely. It was good, really good.

"Wow, now I'm not lost," I said. "And I ran into you in the street again. That's incredible that we keep doing that."

"Yeah, it kind of is," Ruth said. Her voice still had that odd low and nasal quality, which was such a relief to me because without it she was much too perfect and it would've been too much to deal with her.

"It's like, as opposed to other people, I don't have to worry about losing you, cause we'll just run into each other again."

We walked along Bedford, weaving in and out of the throngs of guys and girls who looked like they were headed for band practice or to their jewelry studios or to jobs working for fashion photographers. They sort of made me feel like the new Y-3 neck warmer I'd picked up at Barneys Co-Op wasn't as cool as I'd thought.

"This scene is intense," I said.

And Ruth nodded. She grabbed my hand. She

was wearing tall pointy boots and a miniskirt and a shredded leather jacket with a bright orange shirt underneath that had a high collar. Her honey-colored hair was down and flowing.

"Do you live here?" I asked.

"No—I live in this old loft in Nolita with my parents, on Mulberry Street across from Saint Valentine's. But I'm here all the time. I worked at the Bell Café last summer, but I still like to hang out there even when I'm not working."

"That's cool," I said.

We got to the Bell Café and went to the back garden, even though it was cold back there. They had a bench with a stone table in front of it and she nestled close to me. The sun was low, but it found its way to us through the scraggly trees.

"What about you—where do you live?"

"I live with my mom, but she's away right now. So I'm staying with my friends."

"I met them the other night."

"Well, you met two. There are two more."

"Five of you."

"Except one of us is Patch and he's never really around."

"Where is he?"

"He's lost."

She smiled. And then we were kissing on the bench. And I was happily alone with her. Or we were alone together. Or it didn't matter. I'd met a girl at a party who I'd already had electricity with on the street so it felt like fate, and we'd clicked against all odds of that happening, and now we were kissing and I wanted to never be with anybody else again but her.

"I don't know what it is," she said.

"Yeah."

We stayed there until it was pretty dark, huddled together in the back of that café. Music came from inside, Velvet Underground, and it was like the whole feel of being with her, warm and trusting and extremely cool. She made me feel good, so good I had completely forgotten about all the trouble with my dad, and all the trouble I sensed was somehow brewing with my guys. After a while though, she said she had to get home to hang out with her parents before going out with her friends. And I had to get back to Arno's.

"When can I see you again?" I asked.

"I don't know," she said. And she was suddenly uncertain. Now that it was dark it was kind of cold, so we stepped inside the Bell, where they were transitioning from daytime coffee spot to nighttime bar. I tried to keep looking at her eyes, but she was looking around.

"What?"

"Let's not schedule anything. Let's just talk later, okay?" Her voice was so imperfect, and I just can't say enough about it—what a relief that single imperfection was. I took up her honey-colored hair, touched her neck, and kissed her once, slowly.

"Okay," I said.

## dinner with the wildenburgers

Patch's parents, Frederick and Fiona Flood, were at Arno's for dinner, along with a completely nondescript pair of Arno's dad's business friends. Arno sat and drank wine with them in the living room. Everyone was on two couches, facing each other, except for Arno's dad, who remained standing. Arno knew his father liked it when people had to look up at him.

It was Tuesday night and Arno was enjoying himself, getting a little buzzed on the wine and vaguely following the gossip his parents so enjoyed exchanging. He didn't tell a lot of people about it, but he kind of got a kick out of hanging out with his parents. This was never true when they were alone, because then their relationship showed too much wear, but with other people, they put on a good show. Right then they were talking about their escapades in Florida.

"And when the maid caught us in the pool, in our birthday suits no less, she sang us a song! Isn't that fun?" Alec asked.

"Lord, Alec. She was praying," his wife shook her head and finished her wine. The front doorbell rang. "Someone go get it," she murmured, half to herself. Arno stared at his mom. She was unbelievably pale in a black sheath dress that accented her thin wrists. Her black hair swayed around her head like a mini motorcycle helmet. If he hadn't seen her naked by the pool with his very own eyes just a few weeks ago, when he'd been obsessed with Jonathan's cousin Kelli, he'd never have believed she was capable of that sort of thing.

Jonathan passed by the huge living room. Arno saw him stumble. He must not have realized there was a big dinner party happening, and he just kept going.

"Hey," Arno said. Jonathan peeked into the room and motioned that he couldn't deal with the scene just then, but that he'd be back in a second.

"Alec, would you recommend we buy another Pardo sculpture for our land in Connecticut, something for our north lawn?" Frederick Flood asked.

Arno watched his father stiffen. And he was pretty stiff already in his blue corduroy suit, a silky pink shirt, and black velvet loafers with fox heads embroidered on them. His mom, who had been looking pretty relaxed, begin to fidget with her big sparkly diamond wedding band. In a faraway room, a phone rang.

"I think Ricardo Pardo's work may be . . . no longer

so fashionable," Alec Wildenburger said, looking at his wife and frowning. "In fact, I'd sell my Pardos, if I were you."

"That's disgusting of you to say," Allie snapped at him.

"Come now, Allie," Frederick Flood said. He stood up and put a hand on her shoulder, which she shrugged off. "If Alec Wildenburger says Ricardo Pardo is done, believe me, he is done." He laughed.

"Don't be so sure about that," Allie muttered, and left the room.

Arno finished his glass of wine just as Jonathan walked back into the room. His face was roughed up from having been quickly washed and he seemed, not high exactly, but glistening. Arno smiled. It looked like Jonathan was in love.

"What's up, man?" Arno said. The group glanced over at the two teenagers.

"Everyone," Alec Wildenburger announced, "you know my son's friend Jonathan."

Jonathan blanched slightly when Alec spoke, and gave only an awkward wave. *Weird, weird*, Arno thought. Of course everyone is flipped out by everybody else's parents, but Jonathan, up to then, had always gotten along really well with the Wildenburgers. He had a gift for pretending that he was a little adult and Allie and Alec Wildenburger were the kind of parents who enjoyed that. But now . . . wasn't Alec going to see Jonathan's father in London in like a week? Hadn't someone mentioned that to him? And didn't it have something to do with that PISS woman that was taking him and Jonathan on the sailing trip? Arno had never been a stickler for details, but at the moment he wished he'd been paying more attention over the last few days.

"*Hullo,*" Jonathan whispered. Frederick Flood nodded once curtly and looked away. The other nondescript couple were quiet. Then one said:

"Jonathan . . . haven't we heard something about your father?"

"*Something not so savory,*" whispered the other.

"That's the one," Fiona Flood said, and there was an edge to her voice. She sounded extremely pointed and gossipy.

The bankers looked away. Arno watched. Even his own dad seemed to glare slightly at Jonathan before helping himself to more Camembert and crackers. The huge living room was quiet except for the weird harp music that was playing in the background. A log crackled in the fireplace and a spark flew out, past the grate, and onto the Aubusson rug. Jonathan jumped over and stamped it out. Arno watched in utter confusion as no one thanked him.

"What are you two doing for dinner?" Allie asked. She'd come back into the room with a full glass of wine.

"I guess we're not eating with you all," Arno said, suddenly totally annoyed at his parents and everybody else for being such assholes. So what if Jonathan was staying over for a few days because his mom was a loon and had split town while she was having their apartment painted? And whatever about his dad—what were they even talking about? Fuck them. He'd been totally mellow only five minutes ago, enjoying the relative warmth and safety of his own living room, and now his mom and dad had messed it up all over again. He really wondered what he was going to do with the two of them.

"We're going to smoke up some heroin in my room and watch sadomasochistic porn," Arno said. "You know, chase the dragon and then wag its tail?"

"Very funny, darling," Allie said. "Now get along, you two. On to your mischief."

No one had even offered Jonathan a glass of wine. Arno scratched his head. He didn't get it.

"Okay," Arno shrugged. "See you."

Arno walked out of the room without looking back at his parents or their guests, and Jonathan followed.

They went down to Arno's wing, padding quietly

down the hall.

"Your dad had on velvet shoes with foxes on them."

"I know. My dad is so gay."

"You know—" Jonathan pulled up short and stared at Arno. Arno stared back.

"What?" Arno asked.

"He really is," Jonathan said.

Arno said nothing. They reached his room and he grabbed some fifty-dollar bills from a silver bowl on his desk.

"I was kidding."

"What?" Arno asked.

"About your dad—I didn't mean it."

"Oh. Right—anyway, I don't care. They're being assholes for some reason I don't get. It's like, lately I hate my house. Let's get the hell out of here."

### david is good at football, too

Wednesday was a bright fall day. The sky was an incredible blue and it was a perfect, bracing fifty degrees. With just a week before Thanksgiving, each day that could be enjoyed outside felt like a little gift, and everyone in the city seemed to know it.

Because of the weather, after school David and Mickey made their way to the baseball diamonds in Central Park, where they were going to play football.

It was a weekly game and whoever showed up played. David was always a quarterback because he had laser accuracy and an incredible ability to throw the bomb, and Mickey liked to be a lineman so he could grab guys and wrestle the ball away from them. They hadn't talked since David called Mickey and told him about how Jonathan wasn't supposed to invite them all on the trip, which David was currently wishing he hadn't done, since Mickey seemed very, very on edge.

"I mean, I kind of can't believe Jonathan," Mickey said. He kept shaking his head and looking around. "I sort of feel like he lied to me, you know."

"I know." And David did know. The trip was nothing, but the more he thought about Jonathan's dad stealing that money, the more he wondered if Jonathan knew about it all and was just taking him sailing to keep him quiet about the whole thing. "He and Arno said they were going to come a little later."

"Oh yeah? If they show up, I'll give you twenty bucks," Mickey said. "I love those guys, but they suck at sports, especially team sports."

"I think they're just planning to watch."

"That's lame."

They walked quietly for a moment. They were both wearing sweatshirts, running shoes, and wind-pants, so they made loud swishing noises while they walked. David had a football stuffed in his kangaroo pocket. He looked pregnant. They sipped steaming coffee from paper cups.

"Really fucking lame," Mickey said.

"Hey," David said. "What's the matter? Maybe it's a big misunderstanding and he really did mean to invite you instead of me. Or maybe he's ditching both of us and he picked Arno instead. And we don't even know if he invited Patch."

Mickey kicked at some pebbles in the horse path. "Yeah, maybe."

But David didn't like the sound of that any more than Mickey did.

They arrived at the baseball diamonds and waved at the ten kids who were already there, throwing around footballs and tackling each other. One kid, clearly hungover, was dry-heaving into a bush. Another had already twisted his ankle and was lying on his side, moaning. A few girls were there to play, too. The group of footballers approached them. Mickey and David tossed their coffee cups into a trash can.

"Mickey's got to be on my team," David said to the group. "I don't want this crazy monkey sacking my butt every time I get a snap."

Immediately, a guy from Collegiate named Roman called for Mickey, and Mickey went on the team that wasn't David's.

"I want you!" Mickey yelled and pointed at David. He started hopping up and down and barking. "I'm Ray Lewis and I am going to bury your sorry ass in the dirt!"

"Great." David looked around and saw Jonathan and Arno coming toward the field. They were late, and everyone watched them approach. They were both in long black overcoats, crewneck sweaters, and loafers.

"I have Arno," Roman yelled. "Not the other one."

"We're not playing," Jonathan called out.

"What're you, cheerleaders? Fuck that!" Alex Turner screamed. He was Mickey's team's captain. "I got Arno."

Everybody on David's team was quiet. That meant they had Jonathan.

David watched Arno and Jonathan confer for a moment, and then Jonathan jogged over to David. They nodded at each other.

"Can I stay at your house tonight?" Jonathan asked. "I've had about enough of Arno's."

"Of course you can." But David knew his voice was stiff.

They set up to play, and on first down, David lobbed one out to Jonathan, who did his best to catch the ball. David watched as the ball spiraled and then he saw Jonathan seem to tug it down from the sky. Then everyone stared in complete surprise, as Jonathan brought the ball down and cradled it in his scrawny arms. Mickey launched himself at Jonathan just as he began to run. And Jonathan went down, the ball squirting out of his hands and bouncing away. Mickey and Jonathan landed on the grass.

"Wow," Jonathan said, "I forgot you were allowed to do that!" He tried to laugh as he struggled to his feet, and then extended a hand to Mickey.

"Yeah," Mickey said. "I love to come right at the guy

with the ball—I'm really upfront and honest that way. No lies here."

"Okay," Jonathan said. Mickey looked at Jonathan and saw that he was totally confused. They jogged away from each other, and Jonathan caught Arno giving Mickey a "what the hell, dude, you know Jonathan is fragile" look.

They played a few more downs, and then everyone was huffing and out of breath. Jonathan was bent over, still, from when Mickey had taken him out.

"Let's go!" Alex Turner screamed. Everyone looked at him. He was really into the game. Just then Froggy came up in a brand-new Giants football jersey.

"I want in." Froggy pranced around, and started pointing at Arno, because he wanted to get back at him for breaking his parents' bed.

"You can have my spot," Jonathan said. "I've got to make a phone call. See you guys later. David, I'll be at your house around seven or eight."

Jonathan was already walking away before anyone could stop him. David, Mickey, and Arno watched him go. They turned around and looked at the remaining players. Froggy grabbed the ball and ran with it, and then flipped onto the grass.

"Is he trying to tackle himself?" David asked. While they watched, a knife fell out of Froggy's pocket. He stood up and hid it, and bounced up and down, staring at Arno. While Froggy screamed at Arno, everyone stared at the smear of dog shit he'd gotten on his khakis.

"Can you imagine getting stabbed to death playing pick-up football?" Arno asked. "I don't think I want to play anymore."

"Everybody in position!" Alex Turner screamed. He grabbed the ball and torpedoed it at David, who caught it with one hand and shot it back.

"We're done for the day," David said. But when he looked around, Arno was already gone. David called out to Mickey and they walked toward the park exit together.

"Somebody should call Jonathan and make sure he's okay," Mickey said. "I really creamed his ass."

"Don't worry. I'm going to see him for dinner." David smiled, and the two waved their cell phones at each other.

Mickey was already calling Philippa. So David speed-dialed Amanda. But then he pressed END when he remembered that he was supposed to be getting secretly engaged to her, and he punched in Risa's number instead.

"If my best friend did that, I'd chop his balls off."
Liesel said and laughed heartily, her voice jumping up
and down multiple octaves.

"It's not a joke," Arno said, and to console himself,
he slid his hand along Liesel's naked thigh. He thought
it might be the softest and warmest part of her. They
were in his bathroom, in his apartment, sitting side by
side on the marble bench in his big glass-enclosed
shower. It was early evening, and they were both draped
over with towels and drinking some herbal tea that the
Wildenburgers' cook had made for them and left by the
door.

"I mean, really," Liesel said. "He stayed at your
house and invited you on vacation but then you find
out that actually he's bringing someone else!"

Arno had just explained to her as much as he knew
about what was going on with Jonathan, all of which
he'd heard from Mickey, who had called on his way to
do homework at Philippa's. Mickey had told Arno a

garbled version of what he knew since he was feeling bad, both about tackling Jonathan and the nasty look Arno had given him, so he wanted to explain why he had been so fired up during the game.

Arno knew Liesel was maybe not the perfect person to tell problems to . . . but then again, she was supposed to be his girlfriend. Arno closed his eyes. But then he opened them, because he was just beginning to understand that listening to Liesel without seeing how gorgeous she was, was a very bad idea.

"I need to go home and study," Liesel said suddenly. "You're so naughty, making me act all crazy on a weekday, when I should be home! Everyone was right about you. I have to get out of here. You are so good-looking!"

She kissed him, and for a moment, he felt himself get excited. Then he shrugged her away.

"Man, you change subjects quickly," he said.

"What do you mean?" Liesel asked. "Were we talking about something interesting before?"

"I just want Jonathan to tell me what's going on. And if stuff was normal and his dad wasn't getting remarried right now, then maybe we would just wrestle and like, get it all out. But Mickey made me swear that I wouldn't say anything to him."

"Um, right. I remember when my parents had some friends who got in all this trouble for using the money from the company they owned together to finance their personal lives. My parents cut them off quicker than you can say 'Jack Spratt.' That's how my dad put it. I know it's old-fashioned, but my family doesn't like it when people do things that get them in the papers. Anyway, this couple had a daughter and I never saw her again. I heard they moved to New Jersey and now she goes to public school."

"How is that related to anything? Do you mean you think I should cut Jonathan off because he might bring someone else on this awesome vacation instead of me?" Arno wondered for just a moment if Leisel knew something that Arno didn't.

"I don't know!" Liesel laughed. The sound was braying, and for a moment her nostrils flared. "Sometimes I hear things, but oh well!"

He was glad the bathroom was steamy because he didn't want her to see his totally confused expression.

"Arno?"

They both stood stock still. Through the Liars CD, which was playing plenty loudly in Arno's room, they'd heard Arno's mother's voice calling.

"Yeah, Mom."

"Dinner! Does your friend want to stay?"

"Now I really have to go," Liesel said as she stood up and dropped the towel. Arno's jaw dropped. She was incredible. Too thin, but still incredible.

"I think she's going to go home," Arno said through the door. He stared at Liesel, who was struggling into a silvery-pink bra.

"If you stare too long you'll turn to stone." She giggled, and leaned down and kissed him. Then she sprinted out of the steamy bathroom. Arno followed her, and they dressed quickly.

"Being with you is so fucking *outrageous*." Liesel laughed and looked around for the rest of her clothes. "You are so much more fun than all those rigid uptown boys I've been with!"

"Yeah," Arno said. "Hey, do you want to meet my mom?"

"Are you crazy? We barely know each other—what do you think I want to do, marry you?" Liesel started laughing uncontrollably and threw herself on the bed. And all of a sudden, Arno thought, *hey, I think I kind of like this girl. I don't get her at all, but I like her.*

Amanda called David and his phone vibrated. David saw her name and jumped in the air.

"Don't worry," he said to Risa Subkoff, who was standing next to him.

"I wasn't."

Risa was in long basketball shorts and a T-shirt. She had her long dark hair back in a ponytail and her hands all over David because they were playing one-on-one basketball with unlimited physical contact.

They were in the Reebok Sports Club on the Upper West Side, where Risa worked some evenings as an instructor/semipro for women's basketball, which basically meant that she went one-on-one with career women in their thirties and forties and helped them with their jump shots. Because of this she had free passes, so she and David were on the court, which was a whole lot more modern and fun than the courts at their schools.

David locked eyes with Risa, then went up and

dunked, because he could.

"I found out from my friends all about you and Amanda Harrison Deutschmann and how serious you guys are." Risa took the ball from David and shot from three-point range. She made it. The club was quiet because it was nearly nine on a Wednesday.

"Uh-oh," David said and sighed. What was he supposed to say? He didn't know. That he might be still in love with Amanda and they could probably be happy together if they could just stop cheating on each other? Um, no, he couldn't say that. He took a deep breath and tried to imagine what his dad might say.

"I can imagine that you must be angry," David said.

Risa grabbed David by the front of his Tarheels T-shirt.

"I was really embarrassed the other night," she said. "I'm sure your dad thinks I'm a whore."

"He doesn't think in terms like that."

"You do know that I don't care that you have a girl-friend, right?"

"Um, I'm not even going to try to understand that," David said.

"Good, don't." She was smiling, so David started kissing her. But he knew that no matter what, he wasn't Arno. And that was what this was all about, he realized. Trying to get back at Arno for what had happened a month ago, when Arno had fooled around with Amanda at Patch's house. He still wasn't over that. *Look at me, I can be a cheat, too.* But it wasn't working. He knew it, he just wasn't ready to admit it yet.

Then Risa pushed him away and they played a slow game of one-on-one. Some adults stopped to watch as they came back from their massages and weight training.

Risa blew past David and went for the hole and David body-checked her. She tripped, and they landed in a tangle on the floor. He kissed her. Amanda would never play with him like this. It would mess up her hair. But for some reason he loved that about Amanda, that holding back thing she always did. And there, in the warm glow of the basketball court in the Reebok Club with Risa, who was so right for the room, he was thinking only of Amanda and how to get back to her. And he hoped against hope that she wasn't doing the same thing he was right then.

## mickey is suddenly left to his own devices

"I don't understand why we can't get fucked up," Mickey said. "I mean, I'm kind of tweaked about this stuff with Jonathan. I sort of always thought we were the closest, you know? And now I find out he's lying straight to my face."

"And plus, you were really excited to go do some wild stuff since we've been acting so calm, huh?" Philippa said.

"Well," Mickey looked at his girl and remembered again how amazing it was that she could totally read his mind. "Yeah, that's true."

He sat with Philippa in a back booth at Man Ray, and he had an ice pack on his ear from when he'd smashed into Jonathan at football. The Neptunes were playing, so the room was really loud, and it was also kind of dark. Philippa had her hair pulled back and she was looking particularly prim. And Mickey was trying to relax into his role as a happy boyfriend, but he also wanted to get a little drunk and it seemed as if Philippa was telling him he couldn't do both.

Philippa's phone buzzed and it was Liza Komansky, who was currently defiantly incommunicado from everyone in the group, but who was still kind of obsessed with Jonathan even though she said she hated him. Philippa answered and immediately they started talking about Jonathan.

"And apparently, Jonathan has a new girlfriend, on top of everything else," Philippa said into the phone.

"Don't tell Liza that." After all, Mickey had only heard that secondhand from Arno, and this rumor stuff seemed like it was getting out of control.

"Why not?" Liza yelled back through the tiny speaker. "I don't have a thing for him. And you tell your friend Jonathan that I don't care if his new stepmom could buy her own country, I still wouldn't like him."

"What? How does she know that?" Mickey asked.

"Come as soon as you can," Philippa said to Liza, then she hung up and turned to Mickey. "Word travels fast. Plus, she said she saw Jonathan at Barneys buying a weird neck warmer and talking to a salesgirl about what the best deck shoes for a five-hundred-foot yacht would be."

"It's not five hundred feet."

"Well, anyway, that's what she said." Philippa flipped her hair.

A waitress came by and delivered plates of crab cakes and tall glasses of cold beer. She winked at Mickey, and Philippa saw.

"Watch it," Philippa said to the waitress. Mickey gave her a half frown. He'd known the waitress since he was eight or so, and she'd seen him in all sorts of states. She was a cellist who worked only a few nights a week. Her name was Diane, and Mickey had only fooled around with her a couple of times.

"Think of me as a cousin," Diane said to Philippa.

"When Mickey went to Brazil he slept with two of his cousins," Philippa said back.

"Oh." Diane reddened and walked away.

"I almost killed Jonathan today," Mickey said, tearing into his crab cake. "I still can't get over the trust thing. I mean, if it was Patch, or even Arno, I'd just figure it was an honest mistake, but Jonathan is way too uptight to not realize he's invited us all even though we're not all allowed to come."

Philippa sighed and looked at Mickey in sort of a bored way.

"There must be something else Jonathan's not telling us." Mickey spoke with his mouth full, and twisted his finger in his ear. He'd said it, sure, but he couldn't follow his own reasoning. Then Mickey got even more tangled in his thoughts, because now he felt like he was doing Jonathan's job, which was figuring out all the gossipy-shit. And this was not a job he was particularly good at. He looked at the restaurant's gigantic front door and suddenly it opened and Liza came sweeping through it. She was dressed all in black and her flowing coat slapped the backs of other diners' heads as she passed.

"Well, here I am," Liza said. She kept her coat on and sat down next to Philippa, who immediately started whispering to her. Mickey shrugged at both of them and started drinking Philippa's beer, since he'd finished his own.

"Can I get you anything?" Diane asked Liza. Everyone looked at Liza. The only thing colorful about her were her eyes, which were red and puffy. She just shook her head and sniffled.

"You're tearing yourself apart over Jonathan, aren't you?" Philippa asked, and stood up. "Mickey, I love you, but I've got to go take care of Liza."

"What am I going to do?"

"Finish your dinner and go home and do your homework," Philippa said. Liza helped Philippa with her coat. "And don't let me hear that you stayed here all night flirting with the waitress." Philippa leaned in and kissed him, and then she put a protective arm around Liza. Even Mickey could see that Liza was upset.

Everyone knew her thing for Jonathan was quite real.

"I'll miss you," Mickey said.

"I'll call you at eleven and tuck you in over the phone," Philippa said. She straightened her cream-colored cashmere coat, swept back her hair, and followed her friend out of the restaurant.

Mickey smiled at Diane, who still stood there looking at Mickey, now alone in the booth.

"Well, it looks like someone needs to finish up their dinner and go home and do whatever homework gets assigned to boys in their junior year," Diane said. She reached out and pushed her hand through Mickey's thicket of messy hair.

"That's exactly what I'm going to do," Mickey said, nodding vigorously. "But first could you get me a double shot of tequila? I'll have it with a piece of warm apple pie and then I'll go straight home and do my schoolwork."

"That's my little Mickey," Diane said, and went away to put in his order.

# the psychologically convoluted interior world of the grobart family

## a portrait of the grobart clan in repose

"We're not going out to dinner?" David asked his mom. It was nearly eight o'clock on Wednesday evening, but Jonathan hadn't arrived at the Grobart's yet.

Hilary Grobart looked up quickly from the *New York Times* crossword puzzle she was completing. The radio was tuned to a classical music station, and choral music surrounded them. Both Hilary and Sam Grobart were in their big leather easy chairs with their feet up; Hilary with the puzzle, Sam totally absorbed by *The New England Journal of Medicine*. The corners of David's thick lips pointed down. If he could have freeze-framed his childhood, this would be the picture.

"Why, no. Why would we?" she asked.

David tried to remember the last time she'd ever answered a question without asking a question. He couldn't. Her book *Always Ask First* was still hovering in the top one hundred on the *New York Times'* extended list.

"Because Jonathan is coming over."

"All the more reason to have a nice warm dinner at home, don't you think?"

"No."

"David." His mother raised an eyebrow. "Is there something you'd like to share with us?"

"No."

The intercom buzzed and the doorman said he was sending Jonathan up. A moment later there was a knock on the door.

David's dad leapt to attention. He ruffled himself like a pigeon and his eyes seemed to brighten. David watched his dad and a shiver shot through him.

"Hello, Jonathan, dear boy!" Sam Grobart grabbed the door and opened it wide for Jonathan. Johathan put his bulging garment bag and an extra RL bag right by the door, as if he wanted easy access should he need to make a quick escape.

"What the hell?" Jonathan mouthed to David. David shrugged.

"We're very glad to have you here," Sam said. The buzzer rang again, and everyone jumped as if an electric current had shot through the air.

"What the hell is that?" Hilary asked.

"It's the pizza man!" Sam tripped over Jonathan's bag and kicked it as he ran to open the door. A short man in a white apron stood there with two large pizza boxes. "Molto grazie," Sam said. "Everybody loves Lombardi's!"

Sam thrust three twenties at the pizza man, grabbed the pies from him, and shut the door.

"Let's eat here in the living room, it'll be fun!"

"Why?"

"Not now, Hilary. Go get some Cokes."

"You know perfectly well we don't keep soda in the house. Don't you?"

"Oh, right." Sam stood suddenly and ran back to the door. The short man was still there. He handed Sam a six-pack of Coke and Sam slammed the door again.

"Plates, napkins, no forks. This is fun, right?" Sam opened one of the boxes and the smell of mushroom and onion pizza filled the room.

"Don't ask me what's going on," David mumbled to Jonathan.

"*I think I can guess,*" Jonathan whispered.

"Everyone in a circle." Sam dragged chairs around the coffee table and Hilary distributed plates and paper towels. Soon they were all eating loudly. It was really good pizza: thin crust, with fresh mozzarella and basil and garlic you could actually taste.

"Thanks," Jonathan said, between bites. "This is good."

"What life is about," Sam Grobart announced and stood suddenly, wiping his mouth with a paper towel.

"Oh no," David said.

"Life is about forgiveness. It's about embracing your enemies."

"While we're eating?" Hilary Grobart said, closing her eyes.

"It's about breaking bread with those who've hurt you."

"Um," Jonathan said.

"We're okay with the past," Sam waved a limp pizza crust at this audience of three. "But I think we should all be able to wrestle with the fact that your father is a thief, because nothing, nothing, is more important than honesty. I mean really, would we be decent people if we cared that your father stole our money? I for one, think not."

"I didn't—"

"Be quiet now, Jonathan. We love you, see? We are beating our swords into ploughshares!" Like some crazed cartoon maestro, Sam Grobart whipped the air with his pizza crust.

"Dad?"

"Some people keep secrets hidden, but not me. I'm totally against secrecy, which is the enemy of honesty!"

"Is this insanity really some misplaced jealousy of

the success of my book?" Hilary asked her husband. "Because we both know I'm having a lot of trouble with the second one and that must be some consolation to you."

But Sam Grobart, potbellied and bald, with the wild eyes of a street-corner preacher, was beyond hearing.

"The sins of the father are not reflected on the son. Not at all! And we are here, breaking pizza with the son! He shall sleep under our very roof."

"I think I better go," Jonathan said.

"Not without me," David said.

The two boys stood up and made for the door.

"We know everything about you, and we're okay with it! That's what you need to know." Sam Grobart rushed at Jonathan and hugged him. "We want you to stay here for as long as you like. I've been your mother's therapist since before you were born and this is where I've arrived, at a place of complete forgiveness—a place where we all can live in harmony!"

"Calm down now dear, you can't charge anyone for this session." Hilary Grobart pried her husband off Jonathan.

"I forgive, and I share secrets."

"I wish you wouldn't," Jonathan said.

"Boys, don't leave," Sam went on. "There's more pizza and goodwill where this all came from—have another Coke."

But David and Jonathan were already out the door and into the elevator.

"I'm sorry." David looked wide-eyed at Jonathan. "I wish he hadn't . . . you know . . . done that."

"I guess my dad took some money from your dad, huh?" Jonathan wiped at a spot on his coat that Sam Grobart had put there with his greasy hands.

"I don't entirely get what he was talking about, so who can say for sure? My dad can get pretty crazy. I think he's starting some kind of forgiveness sessions. He already has people signing up. I hear Arno's parents are interested."

"That makes sense." Jonathan sighed. They went out of the lobby, and stepped into the windy street. They walked west on Jane, with no particular direction in mind.

"Jonathan?"

"What?"

"Could you not tell anyone that my dad is kind of insane?"

"Okay. But could you not tell anyone that my dad probably did something really awful with your family's money?"

"Okay." David looked away. "Dude?"

"Yeah?"

"Who are you really taking on this sailing trip? 'Cause I think everyone—well, maybe not Patch, because we can't find him again—but everyone else thinks they're going, but I know you said you could only bring one guy, so . . ."

Jonathan sighed. "Yeah, I kind of made a mess with all that."

"And none of us were going to say anything, but I think you need to be honest with us, you know?"

"You sound like your dad."

"I know. It's creepy." David shuddered.

"I can't believe I'm going to stay at your house tonight," Jonathan said. "Do you have a lock on your door?"

"Not really. But we can always prop a chair."

**what the hell is happening in my apartment?**

After school on Thursday I banged on home for a sec to grab some clothes and check to see how much damage had been done. I was basically feeling okay right then, since David had called me out on some stuff, knew about my dad, and obviously didn't completely hate me since he still wanted to come on this vacation. And really, after how cool he'd been, I really wanted him to come, too. But I held myself back from saying it at the time because wasn't that exactly how I'd gotten in that part of this predicament in the first place?

I went to grab a cab outside school, but then I decided that I was still thinking about this hot green corduroy blazer that I'd seen in the window at the Ralph Lauren store at lunch. I was pretty sure that Arno was right and that he couldn't pull off that kind of bright green, but it got me thinking about who could, which made me think, why not me? So I shot up there and bought the very-green blazer that I was pretty sure would look great at a fancy dinner in St. Barth's, but knew I'd never hear the end of from whichever friend I decided would join me on this trip. Except maybe Patch, who was the one guy who didn't really make fun of me and the one guy I hadn't already invited, so go figure.

I got home around four and asked Richard the elevator guy what was up.

"A painter paints." He shrugged his thick shoulders in his uniform and wouldn't look at me. "A painter paints and disasters lurk behind every corner."

"I don't like that."

"Not me either." He let me out at my floor. The door was closed, but unlocked. When I got inside I smelled oil paint and heard laughter. The voice was familiar. A woman. I froze. I knew her. *Oh no.* It was somebody's mom. I turned, slowly, and figured I'd go. But I wanted my clothes. I needed them. There was a pair of pants I'd been thinking about, these good corduroy Polo purple labels that'd get me through tomorrow at least. That laughter: high, trilling, Latin. Mickey's mom, Lucy.

"Hello?" It was the painter, Billy Shanlon, calling out.

"Hi," I said. "I'm just here for a minute." I moved quickly down the corridor to my room, desperate not to deal with them, *in my house*.

"Ey Jonathan!" Lucy Pardo trilled at me. I'd made it to the spot where the corridor opened into our living room and had to stop.

"Look at the fun this Billy is having, eh?" She was basically blocking my way and pointing at the painter, who stood in the middle of the room. Of all the mothers of friends I had to deal with, she was without question the only one who was remotely good-looking. She was forty, *maybe,* with long black hair and easily five-eleven, with heels that made her even taller than that. She towered over me and Billy. I smiled because she was smiling so widely at me. I couldn't remember the last time I'd seen her smile like that. At home, with Ricardo and Mickey always sparring over some nonsense, she tended to look kind of unhappy.

Then I looked at the baseboards in my living room. At first I saw only a bunch of abstract patterns.

"Kneel down," Billy said. He clapped me on

the back. I kneeled down, being careful not to get my clothes too near any paint.

There, around the baseboards, Billy had painted slightly abstracted cubist representations of woodland creatures who were alternately running, or playing, or sleeping, or . . . fucking each other. Bizarre.

"My mother asked for this?"

"She said to have fun with the baseboards."

"And this Billy," Lucy said. "He's very good at fun."

I stood up. Billy had a boom box plugged into the wall and he was playing Latin music: Joao Gilberto. Lucy had her arms up and she was dancing.

"Have you talked to my mom?" I heard myself ask. But Billy and Lucy Pardo had wandered out of the room, headed toward the kitchen. They kept knocking against each other. And then it looked as if they were holding hands.

I left the living room, with its pornographic animals, and went into my bedroom to find pants and shirts and jackets and whatever else might remind me of me and set things right. Billy hadn't even started in here yet, but somehow the room still reeked of paint.

"Hey." Billy had come in behind me. "Listen Jonathan, it is and isn't what you think. But come by later in the week and we can have a talk."

"I think I'll skip that."

Billy smiled. He clapped me on the shoulder. He said, "Sure you are, but you might want to stop by and hang out anyway."

"I just wish you'd stop painting pictures of animals fucking on our baseboards."

"Don't worry. Once you get comfortable with it, it'll seem really cool."

After he was gone I tossed my clothes around for a while, like a salad. I concentrated on Ruth, and her face did the thing in my mind where I couldn't fully see it, which I knew meant I had a huge crush on her, and I couldn't wait to see her in the flesh again.

But the peals of laughter coming from Mickey's mom in my kitchen snapped me back to attention. The idea that I knew where Mickey's mom was and Mickey didn't . . . *oh man*. And the hand holding and what it would no doubt lead to the moment I got out of there—that made me really sick.

## david shouldn't be surprised

"Thanks for meeting me." Amanda stood with David on the corner of West Broadway and Thomas, across from Odeon. It was quiet, and the trees on the street formed a canopy over them. Amanda stared up at David, and hot gusts of breath escaped her lips.

"Of course." David used a sweet voice, and he smiled at Amanda, who was wearing one of her awesome short skirts and white leggings, which she knew he liked. He touched her cheek.

"Have you thought about what I suggested the other night?" Amanda asked. She blinked up at David. She rubbed his arms. She said, "Wow, you're getting so strong."

"Um, yeah, I've thought about it," David said. Of course he had, but he hadn't figured out what to do about it.

"So, we're going to do it?" Amanda said. She glanced at the Odeon, as if someone were waiting for her there. "Look, I really need to know that we are. Because . . ."

"Because why?"

Amanda didn't speak. Expensive cars sped past them on West Broadway, and women walked by carrying tiny yipping dogs. One of the women smiled at David, and Amanda saw. Her eyes went wide.

"You're becoming quite a catch. It's hard to keep up with you," she said.

"Don't say that," David said.

"I need to be in Odeon in a few minutes. I'm meeting my SAT tutor there. I was going to blow off the session, but if you're not going to ask me the thing I asked you to ask me, I guess I'd better go get smart instead."

"Uh, you're taking private tutoring in addition to Princeton Review?"

"Yeah, this is better, he's some guy who really went to Princeton. He works for my dad. There he is."

They watched as a handsome young man in a suit got out of a cab and dashed into the restaurant.

"I'm late." Amanda's voice seemed small, and nervous. "And if you're not going to like, up the stakes with us, I've got to go."

"But don't you think what you're asking for seems kind of unreal?" David asked.

"Sure it is. But David . . . it's like everybody wants you. It's getting hard for me to handle." She took a few steps back from him.

David stared. He waved his hands around, as if he were trying to erase something.

Amanda turned. The light was green. She walked across the street.

"I love you, David," she yelled.

"Wait!"

She didn't look back, though, so David followed her. They reached the front of Odeon, which was Art Deco with lots of warm red light and an overall feel that was not exactly inviting to guys in hoodies and the new And Ones.

"Stop me," she said, as she put her hand on the big brass doorknob.

"Wait," was all David could say. In the back of his mind he couldn't help thinking how bizarre it was that she thought he was so sought-after and confident when he was so totally not.

The Princeton guy must have seen Amanda, because he came to the door and opened it for her. He wasn't a big guy, but he looked about twenty-three and extremely eager to please. David noticed that the guy didn't even bother to glare at him.

"Hello Liam." Amanda passed into the quiet restaurant. David didn't go in. Liam let the door close behind Amanda, and she was gone.

David stood on the street for a few minutes, letting

the cool wind blow his hair around. He couldn't believe Amanda. She was in a restaurant with some junior executive, drinking cosmos and talking about the SATs—all because she thought he was getting too hot. It didn't make sense.

He got out his phone and called Risa, quickly, without thinking.

"I think Amanda doesn't want me anymore," he said, as soon as she answered the phone. There was noise in the background. She was obviously still at school.

"I'm at basketball practice," she said.

"I think I should see you."

David could hear other girls. They were laughing. There was the sound of a ball bouncing.

"Listen, David, I'm not sure about this."

"Why? What about yesterday, with me and you—"

"We were fooling around."

"Well, I know that, but it was pretty good, wasn't it?"

"Yeah, but it wasn't real," Risa said, and it sounded as if this made her happy.

"It wasn't?"

David heard Risa stop, and then whisper into the phone. "Actually, David, I liked being the other woman. It made me feel like a girl. You're the only guy so far who has been gutsy enough to make me feel like a girl."

"But—"

"You and Amanda will get your thing going again. You guys break up all the time."

"No."

"Yes, call me when you get back together with her. Then you can treat me like the other woman again." And Risa was gone.

By then David had made it to Canal Street. From there, it would take him another half hour at least to walk to his house.

Jonathan was in David's room when he got upstairs, listening to his iPod and reading *The Sun Also Rises*. He dropped the book when David came in.

"'We always pay for the mistakes made by others who came before us,'" Jonathan said, and laughed weakly. "Your dad's been in here to see me."

"Not now." David got into bed and threw his pillow over his head.

"What happened?"

David told him, in a voice muffled by the pillow. Jonathan shook his head when David was finished. "I've heard it before. You took on one too many and now you've got two too few."

"Could you not speak in riddles?"

Jonathan was quiet for a moment. David pulled the pillow off and sat up and stared at him. It was seven and the house was quiet. The Grobart parents had just left for a psychoanalytic awards dinner, and they wouldn't be home for hours.

"Come on," David said.

"Maybe you should take some time off from girls."

"Are you kidding? I spent the last fifteen years 'off' from girls. I don't want to take any more time off."

"But you kind of overdid it, don't you think?"

"I'm going to bed." David threw the blanket over himself and turned to face the wall.

"It's seven-thirty on a Thursday night!"

"I don't care."

"I guess you don't want to hear about what your dad said about my dad," Jonathan said.

David listened to him fiddle with his iPod.

"I want my girlfriend," David said.

"Which one?"

"Shut up."

Then David's cell rang. He looked at the screen.

"It's Amanda!"

"See?" Jonathan sighed. "Your problems are totally mundane."

"Hello?" David answered the phone and watched

Jonathan get up and go to the kitchen.

"I just wanted to tell you I didn't fool around with my SAT tutor," Amanda said. "Even though that feeling was totally in the air. I want you to know it was because I can't take my mind off you." Then she hung up.

David lay there with the phone on his chest, his eyes closed. That's when it dawned on him: He just needed to do it. He needed to ask Amanda to marry him, get engaged, whatever, if that was what would make her happy. But he'd have to get a ring on the down-low since if his dad knew, he would definitely find a way to sit David down and explain how this decision was actually about his mother and the fact that she'd breast-fed him for too long or some other creepy psychological theory.

When Jonathan came back from the kitchen with some leftover pizza, David sat up and smiled at him. "How much is a diamond ring?"

"Wha?" Jonathan asked with his mouth full. A diamond ring was maybe the one retail item that Jonathan had never personally investigated. "Well, I guess it depends on if you buy it at Tiffany's or if you buy it in one of those kitchy port towns in the Carib—"

"Yeah, yeah!" David shot up off the bed. "That's it! So I need to come with you. On your trip. To buy Amanda a ring in one of those towns."

I left David at home, where he was lying on his bed drawing ring designs even though I'd forced him to half-admit this was nuts. Outside, I started walking south toward SoHo, then cut east toward Nolita since I just had this feeling like it was time to see Ruth. I was totally relaxed in a laid-back, Patch kind of way. And I was psyched that it appeared like that even to me, though of course it wasn't entirely true, since there was still a lot of stuff going on and I hadn't even attempted to apologize to Mickey or Arno yet. I was a little afraid my vacation apology would come out first and then the "sorry my dad stole your money" thing would spill out right behind it. And I was still holding on to this little sparkly possibility that maybe PISS and all her money was going to make this all go away.

I passed a Korean deli on the way and bought Ruth a bunch of daisies that were the color of raspberry Kool-Aid—which was almost the color of an Etro shirt I'd been eyeing.

Then I walked with the daisies past Café Gitane which was right on her block and I had sudden deep and intense fantasies of Ruth and me sitting in Gitane on a Sunday morning after we'd just gotten up at her house, and her parents were out of town, and we'd be there reading the *Times* and laughing our heads off at how wrong they get everything in the Styles section. We'd kiss in between gulps of café au lait from big white bowls, which is how they do it there.

So I went up the steps and rang her bell and felt a feeling I hadn't felt since several weeks ago when I stopped by the Floods' house to see Patch and only ended up seeing little Flan Flood, who I was really there to see in the first place.

"Heyyy," said Ruth.

She stood in the doorway, looking at me. She was in a pink turtleneck sweater and a long blue-jean skirt, and her hair was held together high up on her head with a leather and wood contraption. The house seemed to blow air toward me, air that smelled of an afternoon that had segued into an evening without anyone noticing because everything was so mellow and good.

"Come on up."

We drifted up the dark wood stairway and passed a big living room with white couches, then a kitchen with lots of cream-colored cabinets, then what must've been bedrooms behind big honey-yellow doors. I'd been in many other people's houses in the last week or so, but this was the first one that made me feel calm.

"It's nice here."

"Yeah, my parents basically work all the time, so I've kind of decorated it myself."

"Wow."

We kept going up, to the top floor, where her bedroom was. She had the new Belle and Sebastian CD on, and there were some candles by her bed.

"I was reading."

"Oh yeah? What?" I didn't sit. She hadn't asked me to. She stood too, but close to her bed.

"This book by Salinger, you know, *Frannie and Zooey*."

"For school?"

"Nope, just for me. I'm re-reading all his stuff." She held out her hand and I took it, because that's what it looked like she wanted.

The next half hour or so was just us on her

bed, fooling around. It was more than good. It was like, *you are my girlfriend.*

When we paused for a second, and before I realized what I was doing, I said, "I feel like there's something I have to tell you."

"You don't have a girlfriend, do you?" I felt her body freeze under me.

"No, nothing like that. But there's this thing I'm dealing with. I need to just like, tell you about it."

"I'm listening."

She smiled at me. Her bed felt so warm, and the way we were lying there was so perfect, like no one could reach us in this place. The door was locked and the big bay windows looked out onto the windblown trees in the backyard, and we were inside where it was safe and warm.

I turned to her. She smelled of perfume and wood smoke. We both did. My eyes flickered.

"Okay," I said. "My father left my mother and moved to London about six years ago. Now he's going to get remarried, to this really, really rich woman. And yeah, I know that's a weird thing to say, but it's important to the story."

"Okay." She smiled, pushed my hair back over my forehead. "Go on."

"Well, my dad, Howard is his name, I guess what happened is he started making investments for all my friends' parents and he blew a whole lot of money for them, but back then everybody was losing money anyway, so it seemed like not such a big thing."

"So what's the big deal? Everyone's parents are kind of embarrassing. That's the nature of the job."

"I know, but it's worse with my dad. Now that he's getting married again he wants to come clean with the world or something, so he's admitted that he stole all that money."

"What money?"

"From my friends, the money that my friends' parents gave him."

"Oh." Ruth's eyes were wide now, and round, like marbles. "Wow."

"So I know that David knows, but I think that's going to be okay, but what's flipping me out is that maybe Mickey knows, because he practically punched me out during football yesterday. So what I mean is, I feel like things are going to get worse for me the more people figure it out. But at the same time, I feel—I don't want to feel distant from you."

"No, it's okay." She did the thing that girls do, where she took up the cashmere blanket that we'd kicked to the bottom of the bed and wrapped herself in it. I knew that meant I couldn't touch her now. And I got her point, that she needed to curl up for a moment and think about me.

"I wanted to get it out. You know, because I suspect—I think people will gossip about it. And you know how gossip is. I'm not a thief."

"No of course not. In fact, it makes you kind of sexy, in a way."

"How?"

She put her head against my chest and the blanket fell off her shoulder.

"Like you're an outlaw."

"Naw." I laughed.

Then we were kissing, and a phone rang. But even though it had the same ring as my phone, which was a nice coincidence, it was hers.

"Hey, Liesel." She sat up in bed and placed her hand on my chest, just lay it there.

"That's cool. Oh yeah? Sure. I guess we could. I'm with Jonathan here. You remember him. No? Arno's friend. Designer clothes, yeah. Okay, we'll meet you there. Fun!"

Ruth looked over at me and shrugged, in soft-eyed apology. Ringlets of her hair fell forward and she lay against me.

"I said we'd meet Arno and Liesel at Schiller's Liquor Bar."

"When?"

"Well, now."

We were quiet for a moment.

"I know we're completely different, but Liesel's my best friend."

"That's cool. Arno's one of my best friends."

I turned slightly and saw her books on a low shelf across from the bed, and started to read the titles. More Salinger, Pynchon, *Frankenstein*, tattered copies of *Emma* and *Madame Bovary*. It's always big when you think you know someone and then you see their stuff and your understanding of them adjusts, like a picture shifting into focus. Now I'd told someone, rather than waiting in fear for them to figure it out. That felt a little better, I had to admit.

"So Arno doesn't know, right?"

I'd heard her question, but I didn't turn, not immediately. *The Little Prince,* the new *Our Bodies Ourselves. The Unbearable Lightness of Being. Goodnight Moon.*

"I don't think so—not unless David told him, which I asked him not to. But then again, if Mickey found out, I don't know who told him, either."

## arno trips out with his uptown girl

Liesel and Arno sat in Schiller's Liquor Bar in a round leather booth. It was a little past eleven and the place was packed. The restaurant was white tile and red leather, with accents of brass. The waitresses had high eyebrows and were beautiful, and the busboys had spindly tattoos on their arms, thin moustaches, and black, greased-back hair.

"It's Thursday, right?" Arno asked.

Liesel shrugged. She had her phone out and was talking with someone called Dirk, who was living at her parents estate in Southampton.

"*Yes, I believe it is,*" Arno whispered to himself.

"Where are they?" Liesel had her hair twisted up in a gigantic bun, with a pair of gold chopsticks through it. "I need a drink. Don't you?" Liesel waved her arms around. When a waitress came by she ordered Irish coffees for both of them. Great, Arno thought, now I'll be slightly buzzed and very awake. "Don't you love this place? It makes me feel so very soigné !"

"Huh?"

"Like, sophisticated."

Arno glanced at her. Of course she was trying to be very grown-up. She'd come from an afternoon of "consulting" for Miss Sixty, down on Mulberry Street. She walked around the store and arranged things and got to shop for a discount, not that the discount mattered at all to her. Apparently downtown stores were very into getting her "uptown" touch.

"Sure."

"Ruth is awesome! Just wait till you meet her. She's extremely retro, and so, so beautiful. It's insane that your friend hooked up with her. What did you say his name was again?"

Before Arno could open his mouth to say Jonathan's name for the tenth time, Jonathan and Ruth parted the red leather curtain that kept the restaurant insulated against the cold breeze from the street and stepped inside.

"Darlings, over here!" Liesel yelled. Then there was much kissing on cheeks and everyone settled in. Liesel ordered more Irish coffees for the newcomers.

Arno pulled Liesel closer to him, and sniffed at her hair.

"Don't yank me!" Liesel picked up a bread knife and pointed it at Arno's throat.

"Down, girl," Ruth said to her friend. Liesel dropped the knife with a clatter and threw her arms around Ruth.

"I love you!" Liesel made a raspberry noise on Ruth's cheek with her open mouth. "And I hate being yanked!"

"These boys," Ruth said, trying to wriggle away from Liesel, "are going to find you annoying if you don't stop."

But clearly, Liesel was long past caring what anyone thought of her.

"So this trip?" Arno asked Jonathan, who was carefully examining a menu.

"Right. I need to talk to you about that." Jonathan put down his menu and leaned in toward Arno very seriously. "I'm only supposed to bring one person. But I asked all you guys, except Patch, and that's mostly just 'cause I haven't seen him, and now I'm kind of screwed because I can't choose between you all like that."

"I get that," Arno said. "I guess you'll just play it by ear and let us know what you decide later?"

"Yeah, I guess."

Neither Jonathan nor Arno looked like they were crazy about that idea.

"Hey—is there something you're not telling me?" Arno asked.

"Can we get some service over here?" Liesel yelled. She grabbed a waiter with a bleached-white mohawk and ordered a bottle of champagne and a lot of tapas, a few pieces of everything.

"Not really," Jonathan said, to Arno. "Or, well, nothing you've got to know now."

"Hmm," Arno said, noticing the way Ruth had just tried to catch Jonathan's eye when he said that.

"Boy, I sure wish I didn't have to go back to David's house tonight," Jonathan said. But Ruth and Liesel were talking and laughing so loudly that no one could hear him.

## this is not who mickey is

"Are you the kind of guy who says no to a friend in need?" Jonathan asked. He'd gone out to the street and called Mickey.

"No, that is not who I am." Mickey laughed.

"Dude, please. I can't stay at David's house any longer. I think his dad is going to make me sacrifice a goat, and David's totally absorbed with designing engagement rings, which is just too weird."

"You want to talk about what's going on with you?" Mickey asked.

"Man." Jonathan hated all this apologizing, even though he knew it was totally necessary. "I fucked up. I invited you and Arno and David on this trip but the problem is, I can only bring one of you."

"Okay," Mickey sighed. "Well, at least you finally told me." He was in his room, listening to some pirate dubs of Moby that one of his dad's assistants had made. "But you still can't stay here till Sunday night, my parents said."

"But it's Thursday!"

"I know, man. And I'm sorry." Mickey really was sorry that Jonathan couldn't stay with him, but his mom had gotten totally sketched out when he asked if Jonathan could stay over. What reason could his mom have for dissing Jonathan? Mickey didn't have a clue. "It's not my fault," Mickey said, into the phone.

"Yeah, right. You're forcing me to stay at Patch's for the weekend and I can't even get in touch with him."

"I don't think he's around."

"No shit!" Jonathan yelled into the phone.

"Um, don't yell. I've got to go."

The two friends hung up on each other. Mickey ambled out of his room, and went down the hall to where his dad was making a series of sculptures out of the chrome bumpers from Cadillac Escalades. They were so clean and shiny they kind of hurt Mickey's eyes and reminded him of a really bright day on the ocean somehow, which made him think of the sailing trip and how Jonathan might not take him, which was definitely a bummer.

Mickey raised his eyebrows at one dude, a new guy called Howie, who had a Triumph motorcycle that he let Mickey use sometimes. But Caselli, Mickey's dad's foreman and Mickey's involuntary caretaker, didn't like this. And Mickey was afraid of Caselli, because he had more or less crowned himself the king of Mickey's many caretakers. It was sort of like having a gigantic, bald, male nanny. So in Mickey's mind, Caselli existed in opposition to his parents, who could be strict enough, but generally weren't around often enough to keep track of what Mickey was doing wrong. So Mickey had had to figure out a code language to use with Howie.

"Will you sell me some pot?" Mickey asked, as loud as he could.

Howie looked around. Caselli was watching.

"Yeah, I will. Here you go," and Howie handed over the keys, but he cupped his hand. Mickey thrust a twenty at him.

"Thanks," Mickey said.

"You're not borrowing his motorcycle, are you?"

"No, I only sold him pot," Howie said, as Mickey scrambled out of there.

"Well, pot's not great, but I guess it's okay," Caselli said. "So long as Mickey stays away from anything with an engine. I mean, someone's got to draw the line somewhere."

Caselli scratched his bald head. All of Ricardo Pardo's assistants wore white overalls and they looked both forbidding and a little futuristic. Mickey looked back at them and nodded a thank-you to Howie.

Outside, he leaped on the old Triumph, gunned the engine, and shot onto West Street. It was only once he was going pretty fast toward Philippa's house that he realized he was only in white shorts and an open pajama top that had fire hydrants and dogs on it. He shook his head. It was barely forty degrees out, and if he hadn't remembered his goggles, he'd be really cold.

When he got to Philippa's block he popped onto the sidewalk and parked in front of her house. A guy in a suit made a snorting noise and Mickey snorted right back at him. Then he ran up the stairs three at a time and leaned on the buzzer. After a while, Philippa came out. She was in a white cashmere bathrobe.

"I was napping," she said.

"Why?"

"Because I was thinking of going out tonight, and I'm tired because you came by at four a.m. last night after you got done at Man Ray so we could discuss our relationship, remember?"

"Oh, right." But Mickey didn't really remember. He tried to smile at her. She didn't invite him in.

"Listen, I need to talk to you about this Jonathan problem."

"Oh, Lordy. Jonathan is not the problem."

"He's not? I thought he was." Mickey shivered.

Philippa still hadn't invited him in.

"No. Your mom is. And your Dad. And my parents. And us. We've got problems. We broke up last night. It all started when I called you at eleven and you didn't answer. You don't remember any of this, do you?"

"No—wait. It was so late. Didn't you come back to Man Ray and we did tequila slammers? Didn't everyone leave and we locked up?"

"No, you jerk! That must've been Diane the waitress! I went home and called you and then I went to bed! Don't you remember when you called me at four in the morning and I came out and sat on the stoop with you and we agreed that the reason we're breaking up is that I'm basically a conservative person and you're basically a complete nutball?"

"No. Come on Philippa. I can't be held responsible for what I say when it's practically dawn. It's how I feel now that matters!" Mickey jumped up and down, as if were trying to readjust whatever was going on in his head.

And then a quiet moment enveloped them. The wind whipped down Perry Street and Mickey looked back at the Triumph, which seemed to shiver. He felt, suddenly, kind of goofy.

"I'm tired of all this wacky shit," Philippa said. "It's over."

"But, I love you."

"I know." She reached out quickly and kissed him hard. And then she stepped inside and shut the door.

## patch has the stupidest outgoing message on his cell phone

*Whup, crinkle, this is Patch, yeh. Leave me a—* beeep.

Hey man it's Mickey. Where the hell are you? Oh, man. I'm in my room man and I just got in trouble all over again for blowing around town on that dude's Triumph. My dad is *pissed.* But I got bigger problems. Philippa broke up with me and I was thinking that we all need to get together, you know? And we need to figure out this thing with Jonathan, like where we stand. Did he invite you on his dad's honeymoon, too? Anyway, I'm around. I need to find my mom and grab some cash off her, 'cause I haven't seen her in like, days. But I'll have my phone with me and I'm not going to lose it. Did you lose yours? If you didn't, call me, would you? You know the number.

*Whup, crinkle, this is Patch, yeh. Leave me a—* beeep.

It's David. Where are you? Me and—um, Amanda. And Risa. I don't have a girlfriend anymore . . . And I'm thinking about buying a ring for Amanda, but I don't know who Jonathan's gonna bring on this trip, so I could use your advice, you know? And there's some other stuff going on with him, but I'm pretty sure I'm not going to tell you about that. Anyway, let's hang out, okay?

*Whup, crinkle, this is Patch, yeh. Leave me a—* beeep.

Dude, it's Arno. I'm like a fugitive from Liesel, man. I need to hole up at your house and do some homework, okay? That girl is out of her fucking mind! I know I should know better than to mess with uptown girls, but this girl is whoppingly nuts, man. I mean I like fun, but this girl *only* likes fun. Anyway, let's hang out. And oh yeah, we need to do something about Jonathan.

*Whup, crinkle, this is Patch, yeh. Leave me a—* beeep.

Hey Patch, this is Jonathan. I need to stay at your house this weekend—or actually, starting tonight. It's a long story and if I can find you I'll explain it to you. But I'm going to come over and bunk in your room, or maybe in the library. If I see anybody in your family when I come there I'll let them know I'm around. And yeah, check in with me. Thanks for letting me stay, man. Even when you're not actually around, it's like, I know I can count on you. There's some weird stuff going on, but, whatever, I'll tell you about it when I see you.

# a few fateful nights at the floods

## who is nicer than little flan flood?

"Patch isn't home," Flan said when she answered the door at nearly one in the morning on Thursday.

"Really? He said he'd meet me here," I said.

Flan eyed my schoolbag, which was looking very heavy, and then she glanced at the garment bag I had slung over my shoulder. It was bulging with all the new stuff I'd been buying for the trip and if I was being totally honest, yeah, I was also shopping to keep my spirits up and, for the most part, it was working.

"What's the story?" Flan asked.

Since Flan and I did have an awful lot of history together, part of me was desperate to share now, to go with her right up to the library, turn the lights down low, play her dad's old Neil Young records and talk about whatever was bugging both of us. And I have to say, being with Flan, even in the doorway, was a whole lot more relaxing than being with Ruth, who I realized just then, for just a moment, felt somehow a little too cool, especially during moments when I wasn't feeling cool at all.

"I've missed you," I said. We hadn't spoken much since I'd gotten involved with that shoe salesgirl from Barneys and admitted to myself and anyone else who might ask that Flan was in eighth grade and hanging with her wasn't cool. Even though that was like, less than a month ago, it felt like a whole lot longer than that.

"That's nice."

Something felt odd. Flan's voice had a pertness to it, a wariness. That's when I saw Adam Rickenbacher behind her. He was the ninth grader who'd swooped in when I wasn't looking and started going out with Flan. But I'd figured it was just a passing thing. And now here he was, inside her house and it was really late at night. And I was still out on the street, holding my bags.

"Look, can I come in? I'm freezing and I'm supposed to meet Patch here later."

"He didn't say that."

"He never says anything. You know your brother."

"Fine, come on in." Flan stepped aside and I

went in and nodded to Adam. I kind of hated that guy. He'd made me look really stupid, and he was only a freshman at Potterton.

"We're in the kitchen if you need anything," Flan said. "There's some food and stuff down there."

And they disappeared. Which meant I had no choice but to go upstairs on my own and figure out where to sleep. I got up to the third floor bedrooms and stopped.

"Patch?"

Silence. Of course he wasn't around. I'd seen him when? Three or four days ago. It was nothing for him to disappear for that long. Frederick and Fiona Flood lived up on a big estate in Greenwich most of the time and let their kids fend for themselves in the city. The big question was whether his parents just straight-up knew about Patch's disappearances and had been deceiving themselves or, even more bizarre, they totally didn't know and assumed everything was fine.

I wandered into his bedroom. A half-eaten blueberry Pop-Tart was on his desk, along with a couple of empty bottles of Yoo-hoo, which Patch drank like it was water. There were clothes and stuff strewn around the floor, mostly dirty jeans and khakis, and no posters or anything like that on the walls. Patch couldn't be bothered with decorating. He was using the spare bed against the wall as a workbench for his skateboards, so there were ball-bearings and trucks and stuff like that thrown all over the greasy comforter. I didn't want to sleep there.

I backed out, into the hallway toward February's room, where I wouldn't be sleeping, since she tended to show up unexpectedly and then she'd terrorize whoever was around. Next was Flan's room, where I'd spent so much time. Not there, either. Patch's big brother Zed's room was pretty much off-limits, since the whole family knew he could be flipping out at Vassar and headed back at any second.

As I wandered down to the second floor, I thought of my brother, up at school with Zed. I'd called him a few times and he hadn't called back. My mom said she'd gotten in touch with him, but who knew the truth. My brother was really into sports and was going to be a biology major. We didn't connect that well.

I stepped into the library, which was really Patch's dad's domain. It was a big room with plenty of leather, books, and all these light-up globes on heavy wooden stands that lit up and rotated if you knew the right switch, which I did. So I got them going and sat down in what felt like a mini Milky Way, and immediately went to work on thinking about Ruth, whom I'd left with Liesel and Arno just a few hours ago. I tried to think about nothing else, not my dad, or who I was going to bring with me on this trip, or that maybe it was a little weird that I'd been spending all this money on my dad's credit card when he'd stolen a lot of that money from my friends' families.

"You okay?"

I looked up. The shiny glimmer in the doorway was Flan. I tried to smile at her, but it's hard to fake anything with Flan. She's thirteen, and very earnest. To me, it always seemed like she was in pajamas. But that was totally wrong. She was in the short gray skirt she had to wear to Chapin, and a black T-shirt she must've pulled on when she got home.

She came in and curled up on the other end of the couch, which put her around five feet from me.

"Where's Adam?"

"Still downstairs. He's playing xBox."

"He seems like a nice guy." I was trying to

sound very mature.

"Yeah. I guess he's my boyfriend."

"Good for you."

"I heard about what happened to you."

Have I mentioned that little Flan has this silvery-sweet voice that's way more special than you'd think a kid could have? Then again, she's also around five foot ten.

"What happened to me?"

"My parents talked about it and I overheard. Your dad got remarried and he's finally coming clean about all the money he stole."

My heart kind of stopped for a second. Of course the fact that Flan knew made the whole thing all the more terribly, horribly real.

"Does Patch know?"

"Nah," she tittered. "You know he doesn't pay attention to my parents."

"Oh, man. I'm probably going to have to leave Gissing. I'm going to move to Brooklyn to hide my face from everyone, I just know it. I'll be one of those dorky kids from Park Slope who spends half their life on the subway." I stood then, and went and concentrated on just one country, Greenland, as it rotated around the top of one of the globes.

"You shouldn't worry so much." Flan stood up.

"Why not?" Underneath my fingers, the Arctic felt smooth and glassy.

"Your friends will take care of you."

"Doubtful. I invited them all, well, except your brother, on this crazy sailing trip with my dad over winter vacation, but I can only bring one of them. Now they're all acting cool enough, but I know it's kind of tense, them waiting for me to choose who I like the best and all."

"Why didn't you ask my brother?"

"Only 'cause I haven't seen him."

"Flan?" It was Adam, calling out. Neither one of us said anything. Then we heard him pad back down the stairs.

"Well, you all have made it this far. And I know you saved my brother. So I bet you can count on them."

"But what if I can't?"

"You have to trust them," she said.

"Why? They're going to hate me when they find out that not only did I overextend my invites, but I'm buying all this new shit with money my dad probably stole from their families."

"Well, Patch once told me that they'd be

nothing without you. They need you. That's how groups work. You just need to be totally honest with them."

"Totally honest? I'm not sure I can handle that."

"Don't you know you have no choice?" Flan smiled and got up to leave the room. "If you lose your friends over this, well, you're an idiot and I'm going to forget I ever had a crush on you."

I watched her, there in the doorway, with the globes between us, all lit up and rotating and valuable and geographically dated and wrong.

"So you're saying I'm acting like an idiot?"

"If you really believe you can't trust your friends," Flan said, "then the answer is yes."

### arno has to make a sudden choice between friends and lovers

"I think Mickey's going to meet us there," Arno said.

It was Thursday night and he was with Liesel. They were headed to a party at Spice Market, on Thirteenth Street. There'd been an opening at Arno's parents' gallery for a new artist called Bolander Berkman, who Arno liked, but Liesel had nixed going. She'd said she wasn't into art, probably because her parents were.

"Mickey?"

"Yeah, my friend. You didn't meet him yet. He just broke up with his girlfriend again last night, and he's pretty upset."

"Oh. Well I hope he doesn't make the whole night mopey."

Arno had taken to wearing a long black cashmere trenchcoat and he had his hands stuffed down low in the pockets. They walked in front of a huge poster for a new play at The Public Theater and Liesel glanced at it without seeming to comprehend what it was.

"I saw *Topdog/Underdog* at The Public with my parents," Arno said.

"What's that?"

"A play."

"Oh. I hope Nina Katchadorian is here tonight. She's awesome."

"What's awesome about her?"

"You have to meet her. She's so funny."

"Why?"

"OH, SHUT UP!"

Arno stared at Liesel. He wasn't shocked at all—she loved to yell in the middle of the street. She loved it when people stared at her. She started laughing hysterically, and ran ahead of him. God she was annoying. And then Arno opened his eyes wide—he'd never quite put it to himself like that before. *Uh-oh.* In a flash he realized that here he was, headed in girlfriend direction with someone he kind of couldn't stand.

"Hurry," she yelled. So they ran ahead. When they got to Spice Market, Mickey was in front of the restaurant straddling a motorcycle. Even though it was freezing out, he was wearing nothing but a black Joy Division T-shirt, torn white shorts, and white combat boots.

"Dude," Mickey wailed, and threw his arms around Arno. Liesel watched from a few feet away.

"I'm Liesel," she said. Then louder, "I'm Liesel." But nobody was paying attention to her.

"I blew it with Philippa."

"Oh man, I'm sorry." Arno kept an arm around Mickey. "Let's get you a drink."

Then Liesel said, "I'm not sure you can get in here dressed like that."

The two boys stared at her.

"It's like, winter and nighttime," Liesel said. "And you're dressed for summer and daytime."

"So?"

"You look like one of the guys who fixes my parents' mopeds at our estate in Jamaica."

Mickey turned to Arno. Mickey was bleary-eyed and at the point of crying. Arno tried to shake his head, to convey, like, *stop, no. I know she's annoying. But I only figured it out about a minute and a half ago.*

"I mean, I'm not sure I want to be seen with you," Liesel said.

"Let's just go in," Arno said. Liesel shrugged and glared. A doorman swept them inside. They were immediately plied with champagne and little crackers with chunks of raw tuna on top, covered with caviar. Arno and Mickey stood there, munching.

"NINA!" Liesel yelled and ran across the room and embraced a short girl who was wearing sunglasses that almost entirely hid her face.

Arno looked around the restaurant. The whole place was decorated to look like the inside of a Chinese opium den, with lights covered in purple and pink fabric, strings of glass beads everywhere, and lots of heavily carved tables and chairs. At the far end of the room was a group of twenty high school kids lolling on dozens of big embroidered cushions, all of whom Liesel seemed to know. They were air-kissing and laughing and braying and spilling drinks all over each other. Several of the girls were openly staring at Arno.

"What the fuck am I doing?" Arno asked, suddenly.

"I don't know, man." Mickey tossed back the champagne and set the glass on a table where some businessmen were huddled. They glared at him.

"Philippa broke up with you?"

"Yeah." Mickey snagged another glass of champagne and some food from a silver plate. He stood there for a moment, chewing thoughtfully, and then he turned to Arno and said, "You know, your new girlfriend was pretty rude to me just now."

"I know." Arno turned up the collar of his overcoat, even though it was really warm in the restaurant. "Wait here for a second, will you?"

Arno moved quickly across the room and got close to Liesel. He tapped her on the shoulder.

"Just a moment," she said. But she grabbed his hand at the same time and rubbed it up and down her back, and then over the place where a normal person's butt would have been.

"Hey," Arno said.

Liesel turned around suddenly. "Could you please wait a moment? We're deciding whether we should all go uptown or not. I think we will, though. This place is lame."

"Well, I'm not going with you."

"Why not?"

"You were rude to my friend."

Liesel smiled. She had an icy quality around her eyes. Arno could see that they were dusted with something sparkly, but it was more than that.

"Well your friend is kind of gross."

"Really?"

"Like, if I were wearing shiny Helmut Lang slippers, he could shine them. Or if I were driving one of those cute new Mercedes two-doors, he could polish it."

Arno burst out laughing. And then he realized he was laughing at himself. Why was he putting up with this person? He didn't even particularly like having a girlfriend, and it wasn't as if looks were the most important thing to him in the first place. Why would they be? He was definitely the best-looking person he knew. Or at least that's what he told himself right then.

"I'm out of here," he said.

"You know what you're doing, don't you?"

"Yeah." Arno took the glass of champagne Liesel was holding, finished it, and handed it back to her. "You're an incredibly wild person. I'm going to miss hanging out with you."

"You're going to really miss what we were going to do tonight."

"I'm not sure that's true."

"Why?"

"Because at the end of the day, even though you're really fun, you're an unbelievably snobby bitch."

On the way out, Arno locked eyes with a few girls. One was clearly a model and Arno had long ago stopped bothering with models. But another was probably part of the random high school contingent who had been invited to the opening, and she looked really nice. Arno thought, *I'm Arno. I'm hot. I'll be okay.*

"Let's go," Arno grabbed Mickey and they made their way out. "It looks like I'm not going back to having one girlfriend in particular for a while."

"You and me both," Mickey said.

Then they went outside and got into an argument over whether Mickey should drive the Triumph home, since he'd managed to slam down about five glasses of champagne in the fifteen minutes they'd been inside. Arno grabbed the key out of the ignition, where Mickey had left it.

"Gimme it," Mickey said.

"No." And then Arno pushed Mickey and his borrowed motorcycle the eleven blocks home.

### my confrontation with old father flood

"So you haven't seen him, Jonathan?" Frederick Flood asked. They were standing in the Floods' kitchen at eight o'clock in the morning on Friday. Frederick and his wife had just come in from Greenwich.

"Who has?" Fiona asked. She glanced around the kitchen, first at me, then at Flan, who was putting on her coat to go outside. Meanwhile the Floods' driver was bringing in suitcases from their car.

The Flood parents were always packing and unpacking at odd times, going back and forth from Manhattan to Greenwich, and then just as often they were headed to Paris or Bermuda or Antigua, or to the horn of Africa for safari. Their lives were a perpetual vacation.

"But you're staying here?" Frederick asked.

"Um, if it's okay." I said.

"Of course it is. It'd just be nice if we knew

where our son was."

"I think he said he'd meet us up in the country before Thanksgiving," Flan said.

"That's this coming Thursday." Her mother sighed and tightened her cashmere scarf around her neck. "Perhaps he'll check in with us before then?"

"I can call him." I pulled out my phone, though I knew how completely doubtful it was that I'd reach Patch.

"No, I talked to him before," Flan said. "He's fine."

"Jonathan, help me take this pot into the garden," Frederick Flood said. I stared at him. He was in lemon-yellow corduroys, a cream-colored cashmere sweater, and Gucci loafers. He wasn't smiling at me. At his feet was a small clay pot.

"Okay." I just sort of stood there, since I couldn't figure how I was going to help him carry the little pot.

"Pick it up and follow me."

"Oh. Okay."

"*Careful*," Flan whispered, as I headed toward the backyard with her father.

The pot was a lot heavier than I'd thought. The

Floods' garden had been planted with the kinds of plants that look good even when they're dead for the winter. We stood there, Frederick Flood and I, puffing air at each other.

"Let me think about where it should go . . ." So while he thought, I wobbled and hugged the pot to my stomach.

"As you may know, I'm a subscriber to the philosophy put forth by our mutual friend, Sam Grobart."

"Oh, God."

"Total honesty, that's my thing. Total honesty, even to a fault. For instance, the moment Alec Wildenburger said Ricardo Pardo's work was over, I saw that he was right and put all my Pardo sculptures up for sale even though I've been friends with Ricardo for more than ten years."

From inside the house we could hear Flan begin to bicker with her mother over whether she had to wear tights to school. Outside, it was alarmingly crisp and the sky was the same stunning blue that it had been all week. It was the warmest November anyone could remember.

"So Sam—my therapist, my counselor, my friend—has confirmed as truth something that I'd long suspected your father had done."

"Um." I looked around the garden, but the wooden fence was easily ten feet high and the stakes were pointed on top. He'd be able to yank me down before I got free. And then he'd probably empty my pockets to get whatever he could to pay himself back for my father's crimes, and then he'd kill me. So even though I knew I couldn't run, I began to back away.

"Can I put this down?"

He didn't look at me.

I heard the front door slam, which probably meant that Flan had left for school.

Sure enough, Fiona Flood came out to the garden. So we were all standing outside in the bright morning sun, and finally I just gave up and set the pot at my feet.

"I want you to tell me the truth," Frederick said.

"About what?"

"How much did he steal from us?"

"How should I know?" I asked. I took another step backward and knocked up against the fence.

"It's not about the money," Fiona said.

"Right. My dad said that, too . . ." But then I decided that probably wasn't the right thing to say right then.

"Well, that's an interesting opinion for him to hold. But yes, it's the principle of the thing. We have tremendous sympathy for your mother. You should know that."

Frederick glared at me. "Talk!" As I scrambled to come up with an answer, we heard the glass door swing open.

"Why, February," Fiona said. "We're busy just now, with Jonathan. Can you—"

"Leave him alone." February Flood winked at me. She and I had been friendly since I'd gotten her into a bona fide private A.P.C. sale a month earlier. And since just a few weeks ago, when she said she appreciated how I handled everything that had been weird with Flan.

"Excuse me?" Frederick Flood turned to his daughter. No two people could have been more different. February looked like Chloë Sevigny after a bad night and Frederick looked like Prince Charles in the middle of a good morning.

"He's a junior in high school and he's going to be late for class and you two are old and mean. If you want what amounts to gossip, you'll have to find it within your own clique."

"Are you joking?" Frederick asked. "We're just having a friendly conversation."

"No you aren't."

I stared at February and her dad. They circled each other, like alley cats about to rumble. I wished I could climb a tree and scuttle out of there. Then, suddenly, Frederick Flood *harumphed* and followed his wife back into the house.

"Wow. Thanks February." I smiled at her.

"Don't thank me—I just get off on screwing up whatever my dad's up to. There's one thing I need from you, though."

"What?"

"Guess."

"Find your brother and make sure he's okay?"

"Exactly. I'm not my brother's keeper—you are. And if you don't find him, I'll unleash the wrath of my parents on you."

"And I can't afford that."

"Right again." February smiled at me, and it was impossible for me to tell if there was a gleam in her eye, or if she was still high from the night before, or brilliant, or what.

"And for what it's worth," she said, "I heard about your Caribbean sailing vacation and I think you should bring Patch. If you can find him, I mean."

"What if I lose him there?"

"It'd be hard to lose him on a yacht."

Then I said, "With Patch, you never know."
And we both nodded at each other.

## i spend friday in heaven

"Tea," Ruth said. We were in her bedroom, which I'd recently decided was my favorite place in the world.

I called her once I'd gotten away from the Floods, and we decided to ditch school. I'd talked with her late the night before and we'd been going on about ourselves. She told me about the car accident she was in with her big sister and her mom a few summers ago, and the year she spent in London when she was in eighth grade and the proper little English boy she made out with there, and the months she spent sailing with her parents in the West Indies, which actually got me pretty excited about this trip with my swindler of a dad. She was so incredibly cool.

"And look, aren't those scones? And jam? This is great," I said. And then I laughed. I was nuzzling her neck and she smelled of the black currant tea and this kind of warm hippie-ish smell that I was getting to really, really like. Even though up to now I'd always said I hated hippies.

"I'm so glad we ditched school," Ruth said. "Especially because we're going away tonight. I would've really missed you."

"You're going away? Where?"

"The Harvard-Yale game. My dad makes us go every year. It's at Harvard."

"Shit! You're going to Cambridge?"

"My sister's a freshman there. We usually have fun when we're together."

"So, you know other Harvard kids?"

"Yeah—Alan Ebershoff's sister is best friends with my sister. Actually I heard that Froggy's been fooling around with your friend's ex-girlfriend—Amanda something? Do I have that right? Describe her."

"Extremely insecure and kind of short—lives in Tribeca?"

"That's her. Froggy will probably be there with his friends, too. They're going to fly up tomorrow morning and they're a lot of fun."

"But I think maybe David wants to marry Amanda. That's why I've got to take him to the Caribbean, to get a cheap diamond." That wasn't the point though. I looked at Ruth. I sighed. "I can't believe she moved on so quickly."

"Some girls are like that."

"Not you, I hope."

"Nope, not me."

I didn't say anything, and for a moment a sharp needle of paranoia and jealousy poked me, even though it was three o'clock on Friday afternoon and we were in Ruth's bed, buried deep under her comforter that smelled like jasmine and hemp. We began to kiss and the Death Cab for Cutie CD on the stereo was like a quiet reassuring whisper, *calm down calm down she likes you she likes you.* And so I did calm down. And then time passed and we must have been sleeping. And when I woke up, I admit, it took me a second to shake off the feeling that sometimes when I was with Ruth, I was kind of pretending to be as laid back and relaxed as her, since no matter how much I wanted to be, I knew inside that I'm not really that way.

"I'm going to the bathroom," I said. "Where is it?"

"Oh, go down to the first floor and use the one there."

"Why?"

"The ones on this floor are these newfangled

kind—my parents discovered them on a trip to Dubai, so they had them installed. But they're weird and guys don't like them. Let's just say they get your private parts extremely clean."

"I don't get it."

"Don't worry about it. Go downstairs. I'll be waiting for you."

"Mmm. I'm really going to miss you this weekend."

She smiled at me. She was half asleep and I watched her. Her eyelashes were strawberry-blond.

When I got back from downstairs, I found some cream-colored paper on her desk and a bit of charcoal and I began to draw her. I didn't do a perfect job or anything, but I managed to get across that her eyelashes were really thick and she had freckles across the bridge of her nose. While I was drawing, she woke up and watched me.

"Is that for me?"

"Of course."

"I made you something, too."

She got up then, and she was wearing this long robe made of all sorts of pieces of silk, a crazy quilt of silk. She looked in a wicker basket by her desk.

"Here it is." She handed me a thick brown wool hat with a white pom-pom on top. It was a little lumpy in places, and the pom-pom flopped to one side like a dandelion by the side of the highway and had some odd straggly bits that made it look misshapen.

"It's for you to wear."

"Really?" I took it from her.

"I knit it over the last couple of days."

I pulled it down on my head and it was immediately warm and I'm sure it made me look ridiculous, but she'd *made it for me.* So it was beautiful. Not something I would ever normally wear, and it would totally not match my new Y-3 neck warmer, but still.

"I won't take it off," I said.

By the time it got dark, we'd decided that I should probably go and she should get some rest before flying to Boston. There was a big dinner that night and she'd probably have to sit next to the president of Harvard. She didn't want to be sleepy for that, since she might want to go there in two years and it'd be worthwhile to try to impress him, even though she'd been told he definitely liked her already.

So I bopped out of her house and onto the streets of Nolita with my new hat on. As I walked toward Fifth Avenue and my apartment, I could feel the pom-pom struggling to sit still on my head.

When I got to my apartment building, there were several people in the lobby, talking. One of them was a short woman in a brown fur coat with a lot of gold jewelry. She was holding a purple folder in her hands and talking to a couple; a man and a woman who had a "just-married" look about them—they were all fresh-faced and scrubbed clean, and they both had pleats in their slacks and black loafers on. I recognized the woman's folder: Corcoran Real Estate.

"It's a classic eight," the fur coat woman was saying. "Rare, very clean, and not even on the market."

There was a shuffling then, as the three of them got closer to each other. And I shuffled too.

"Here's the inside scoop. The family's gone bad—I have that on good confidence from someone in my group therapy—so if we come in and make a hefty offer now, well, let's just say it's a done deal."

"I think we're interested," the man said. He

had that gross heavy-breathing sound that I always associate with new money. But I realized as I slid across the lobby and back out the front door, it was a whole lot better than my own breathing, which just sounded really, really nervous. So a young couple was about to buy the only home I'd ever known because my mom was probably so ashamed of my dad that we'd have to move to Brooklyn after all, just like I'd predicted. Great. I headed toward Patch's and tried to forget what I'd just seen.

**everyone is at patch's but patch**

"We don't know where he is either, but we're going to Greenwich in the morning, and we think all you boys should come," Fiona Flood said to Arno. Unlike Mickey's mom, who was young and wild and possibly having an affair with Jonathan's painter, or Jonathan's mom, who treated them all like little adults, Fiona Flood was just rich and remote.

Arno stood in her kitchen with David and Mickey. They shifted around, waiting for her to set them free.

Fiona went on. "We heard from a neighbor that Patch is up there, and we're not exactly pleased about that, since this is a school week, but you know, we're used to it."

Arno nodded uncertainly. Used to what? That even though Patch was sixteen, he pretty much moved about as he pleased? Or was it that they were used to not being pleased about things. He looked at her thin mouth, at the way her arms were folded over her nonexistent chest. Must be that last one, he figured.

"We think that if we bring all you boys up there tomorrow, he'll show up too."

"Great," Mickey said.

"And with Jonathan already staying with us, it can't be too hard to round you all up."

"Okay," David said.

"Check with your parents, would you? But I'm sure they'll be fine with it. You all have been coming up there with us forever."

"Yeah, since farther back than I can even remember," Mickey said.

"Well, that's taken care of then. See you in the morning. Ten a.m. Why don't you all sleep here? That will make things easier. We're off to dinner at Bouley with . . . David's parents. David, no need to tell them about tomorrow, we'll do it."

She reached for a spare set of keys and tossed them in the direction of the boys as she strode out of the room. Arno caught them.

"Let's go upstairs and make a plan," Mickey said.

The three of them trooped up to Patch's room. When they got to the third floor, they looked around for Flan or February, but neither was home.

They filed into Patch's room, which had the still, delicate air of a place that is rarely occupied. Arno looked around. It was a mess certainly, with a pile of skateboards in various states of repair in one corner and some schoolbooks sitting forlorn and ignored on a desk by the window. The twin beds were equally messy and anonymous. It was unclear which was used for sleep and which was for building boards and storage. The Nakamichi stereo was on, and a Granddaddy CD was playing, low, on repeat. Arno touched the amplifier and it was burning, so he turned it off to give it a rest.

"Maybe we should call Selina Trieff," Arno said. "She might know where Patch is."

"Didn't you hear his mom?" David asked.

"Oh, right." Arno's voice dripped sarcasm. "We're going to Greenwich to be bait, and then maybe Patch will come home."

"Right." Mickey picked up a skateboard that had his name on it, and then dropped it. "God, so much of my shit is over here. Anyway. What about Jonathan? If he's staying here, where is he?"

Mickey and Arno looked at David. David looked out the window at a girl across the street, who was reading on her bed. He missed girls.

"Are we going to talk about Jonathan?" David said. "I think we should."

Fido, the Floods' dog, came running and jumped up on Arno, who was sitting at Patch's desk. Arno hugged

Fido tightly until the dog was barking to be set free.

"Okay, let's." Arno checked his watch. "But I've got to run in a minute. I'm seeing Liesel even though things are definitely over with her. I think we both need to make absolutely sure that we shouldn't be together."

"Or you both want to make sure it wasn't all about sex, and if it was, maybe that's all right," Mickey said. "It's okay, I'm over how she hurt my feelings. And yeah, I've got to see Philippa later at this party for a similar bunch of insane reasons." He grabbed David's arm and checked his Swatch. "Or now, actually." Mickey stood up to go.

"Okay then let's do this fast." David stood up. "I think we need to tell him that he's got to choose who is coming on this trip. Yeah?"

"Fine," said Mickey.

"Sure," said Arno.

Then they all kind of looked at each other, sizing the others up as competition. Sure, Mickey was the most fun, but Arno would definitely find a way to meet girls down there, and David probably was actually closer to Jonathan than the other two. It was anybody's game.

"Well, I guess I better see Amanda again," David finally said. "I know she's at home, because she has SAT prep in the morning. I'm going to try to get back together with her, even if means doing this crazy thing that I haven't even told you guys about—"

But Arno and Mickey were already streaming down the stairs and they didn't hear him.

Out on the street, Arno passed Jonathan, who was headed toward the Floods'.

"I'll be back in an hour," Arno said. "We're all going to Greenwich tomorrow to be bait for Patch."

"Okay," Jonathan said. "Where are you going now?"

"Me and Liesel broke up—but I need to go see her for a few hours and make absolutely sure it was the right thing to do."

"Got it," Jonathan said.

## mickey's one and only true love

"I hear Jonathan's girlfriend's parents are international lawyers and that's kind of complicating things for them," Philippa said. She was dressed entirely in cashmere, in various shades of dark brown. She looked like a cross between Elizabeth Hurley and the world's most beautiful seal.

"Enough with the rumors, baby."

"Don't baby me."

Mickey and Philippa were sitting on a couch at someone's party—a girl named Charlotte Brackett who went to Philippa's school and lived in a converted firehouse on the Bowery. The girl's father was an artist who'd had a fistfight with Mickey's father at a Whitney opening a few months earlier, so Charlotte kept walking over and talking abstractedly about peace and unity with Mickey, but of course he was oblivious and had no idea what her problem was. Charlotte had on a green felt jumper, so she looked like a bit of a Peter Pan character.

"Fine. Is everyone meeting us here?" Mickey asked.

"I doubt it. I hardly know anyone here."

"Huh?" Mickey stared at Philippa, and was suddenly utterly confused. "If you don't know anyone, then what are we doing here? I thought we were supposed to be done with parties anyway."

"I just chose it because it's neutral territory. I can't be alone with you. We broke up." Philippa smiled a heartbreakingly soft and broken smile at Mickey. He was now in a black T-shirt that said DEMOCRACY SUX on the front, and a pair of red canvas shorts, and black motorcycle boots. It was forty degrees out. Philippa rubbed her thick scarf over his arms and smiled at him.

"You could also say—" Mickey searched for words. "That this is our last chance."

"No. Everyone tells me I'm not crazy enough for you. I have to admit that they're right. I can't take how wild you are. Not anymore."

"I didn't cheat on you with that waitress."

"That's not the point. I wanted to be able to call and tuck you in. But you were nowhere near home. Mickey, that made me cry."

They were quiet for a moment. Even though they didn't know anyone at the party, the people hanging around seemed to know who they were. In the other room, the kids were all chasing a half a dozen piñatas that were meant for a kid's birthday party. A bunch of guys had hockey sticks and baseball bats. They'd put on some old Metallica CD and were starting to chant. Normally, Mickey would have been right in there with them, but instead he kept staring at Philippa. Because he had no memory at all of the night he'd disappointed her, he felt even worse that it was coming between them.

"I guess when you're really in love, you have to break up a few times before it takes," Mickey said.

Mickey looked down at Philippa. Tears were streaming down her cheeks. She said, "You're crazy, you know that. But sometimes even when it sounds like you're just talking shit, what you say is really true."

"It only sounds that way when I'm with you . . ." He trailed off.

"Let's stay broken up though, okay? Please?"

"But why?"

"It's like, I love you, but I don't always want to feel disappointed by you. I can't take that anymore. Like, right now, I know you want to blow apart those piñatas with those guys—I don't want to keep you from that."

"Really? I didn't even notice them. Look, what if I promised not to do any more wild stuff?"

"I think we already tried that. And besides, this'll be good. It's almost winter break and then I'll be in Nice with my family and you'll be on that giant boat with Jonathan and we'll both have some distractions."

Mickey snorted, but Philippa didn't need to hear him say again that Jonathan might not take him. Then they didn't speak. And Mickey began to understand that it was really and truly and finally over. Not that it contradicted the fact that they were totally in love. He brought his foot up and kicked a tiny bronze sculpture of a naked boy off the glass coffee table in front of them. Charlotte Brackett immediately skipped over to them.

"Can't you see that I specifically put all the fun and destruction in the other room?" she asked. "Now if you can't play nicely with the other boys, you'd better leave." Mickey thought it was kind of too bad she was yelling at them since she seemed pretty and had a nice tilted nose.

"Me, too?" Philippa asked.

"Of course not. But this violent asshole has to go."

Mickey sighed. He'd been sober and serious for far too long. He kind of thought that he wanted to leave anyway. And he was pretty sure he'd said the one smart thing he wanted to say, though he couldn't exactly remember what it was now.

They walked out through a corridor that was a dozen feet wide and lit by a flashing neon painting that flickered between the words Fate and Jiminy Cricket, which Mickey dimly recalled his father making fun of at a dinner party when he was eight. Charlotte Bracket ran after them.

"I'm sorry I'm so sensitive," she said. "Usually I'm really kind, but it's hard with all this expensive art around."

"That girl's awfully talkative," Philippa said.

Mickey tried to touch Philippa's hand, but she pushed him away.

"I wonder how David is doing," Mickey said.

"Why?"

Mickey tried a smile. He knew that he never said things like that, so he was sure it would get her attention.

"Well, when I left him he was going over to Amanda's house to do basically what I just tried to do with you."

"Oh?" Philippa's eyes widened. She reached forward and grabbed a few white M&Ms from a bowl by the front door. "Are you sure?"

"It couldn't go any worse for him than this has for me."

"No," Philippa said. "It actually could."

## amanda is studying, dammit!

"Really, David," Amanda said. "You might have called first. I'm studying."

She had her little fist cocked on her little waist as she stood in the doorway of her parents' massive Tribeca loft, which looked like a house in the English countryside.

"But isn't this more important? I'm ready to do what you asked me to do, I think."

"Well . . . come in for ten minutes and we can discuss it. Just because you got fifteen-forty the first time doesn't mean you should feel free to diss the rest of us who don't have your brainy genes."

"I'm not. I offered to help."

"You get so impatient. It's impossible to study with you."

David was quiet. It was true. Amanda was really, frustratingly awful at math. They went into her living room, which was filled with overstuffed couches and paintings of someone else's ancestors. What little light there was came from tiny lamps set on end tables.

Amanda sat down on the couch across from David and straightened her white sweatpants and her pressed Oxford shirt.

"You took so long to think about it," she said. "I guess I figured . . . I thought you didn't want to ask me. But I still want you to. Then we'll be able to really trust each other."

David let his head fall to the side for a moment. She'd spoken awfully loud. He looked to his right, but the apartment was set up so that you couldn't see any one room from any other. Jonathan had visited once and said the place had really bad feng shui.

"Okay, are you ready for me to ask? Because the thing is, if Jonathan decides to bring me on this trip to the Caribbean—which I'm pretty sure he will—then, well, we can make this really official." He was shaking.

"Yes, I'm ready to get engaged." Amanda practically yelled. "And then neither of us will cheat anymore."

"Okay, but remember, you cheated on me first, with my best friend."

"*I would not call Arno your best friend.*" For some reason, Amanda had come over and sat on the couch, and she was whispering. David twitched his nose. What the hell? She was yelling before.

David yelled, "Whether or not he's my best friend,

216

you fooled around with him!"

"*Shhh!*"

David stood suddenly. "Maybe this whole idea of getting secretly engaged is insane."

"Could you shut up?" Amanda was standing too. "If you can't understand that I need us to do that, you can't understand anything at all. It's simple, we'll get engaged and then I'll stop—"

"Stop what? Cheating? You still are, aren't you?"

David could feel the tears well up.

"I just want my Yale sweatshirt back, then I'll go."

He walked quickly to the closet in the hall and yanked it open. Amanda was right behind him.

"I want you to go!"

"My sweatshirt!" He ran down the corridor toward her room.

"No!"

He pushed the door and it gave too quickly, as if someone had been leaning against it and had suddenly jumped back. The door swung open, and there, sitting in a chair, was Alan Ebershoff.

"Froggy?" David asked. He was so shocked that he sat down with a thud on Amanda's bed, where the covers were still warm and mussed from whatever they'd been doing just a few moments before.

"Don't call me that," Alan croaked. He wore khakis

and one of those multicolored striped shirts that can only be bought at Brooks Brothers. David couldn't believe it. The kid brushed back his hair. He was kind of fat and his breath was labored.

"I didn't even know you two knew each other." David held out his hands, palms open, to Amanda. She stood in the doorway, twitching her nose.

"Everybody knows each other. You think the uptown kids live in a different country? In a cab at night it's like twenty minutes to uptown."

"The subway is faster," David muttered.

"If you could've just done what I asked . . ." Amanda trailed off, and looked up at David.

"I shouldn't have to ask you to marry me just to keep you from fooling around with other guys." David stood slowly. "I was going to buy you a ring and everything in one of those island towns, though, you know. Just to make you happy." He could see the sleeve of his sweatshirt peeking out from under Amanda's desk. He got down on his knees and retrieved it. The silence in the room was cut only by the radiator, which squeaked and swooned as if it were absorbing the pain of all three of them.

"Hey, you want a bong hit before you go?" Alan asked.

"No. Take an extra toke for me. I know my way

out," David said. "And do me a favor and don't marry her, okay? She asked me first."

He heard Amanda's muffled voice behind him as he moved swiftly down the corridor. Around him, the recessed lighting glowed softly. David shook his head. He did kind of love Amanda. He only wished she was a little more confident. And he frowned at himself, since he knew he was way too young to understand that about her.

"Suck it!" Liesel screamed. She hammered on the table with both hands.

Arno stared at her. Weren't they not getting along? Hadn't they broken up?

She shoved the lemon farther into his mouth. He focused on the bottle of Stoli between them and wished that Liesel was into something mellower, like pot or Vicodin, or Ecstasy. But nothing doing. She liked hard alcohol, very cold, and in large quantities.

They were in a back room at the Daze Inn, a new club on West Street. The Daze Inn catered to entertainment types in from L.A. who were into making sure absolutely everything they did was very expensive and illegal. Liesel had an uncle who owned a piece of Interscope records, and he'd given her his private pass.

"Ready for more?"

"I guess." Arno didn't really feel like drinking, but it was nearly midnight, and he didn't have to be anywhere but back at Patch's house, and that wasn't really till tomorrow morning. He sighed. They had a semi-private room, which meant they were cordoned off from the crowd, but people could see them do shots, which were definitely going to turn into body-shots if things kept going.

Liesel threw back her gigantic mass of blond hair. She groped for the bottle, poured herself a shot in a painted gold glass. She threw it back and nearly flipped out of her chair.

"Now make me suck it!"

So Arno grabbed up a lemon and shoved it at Liesel's face. She sucked. After a few seconds she spat the sucked lemon onto the floor and it bounced out onto the dance floor, where some guy picked it up.

"God my parents hate it so much when I say suck. It's so good to say it a lot. I fucking love you, Arno Wildenburger, you know that?"

"But we can't stand each other. We can't even agree on what color white roses are."

"Or a jet-black BMW X5. I know." Suddenly Liesel nodded very seriously. "It's true. We don't get along."

"Maybe we should really call this thing over, you know? Especially after the fight we had about my friend Mickey."

"There's just one thing."

"What?"

Liesel picked up the bottle of vodka and sipped from it, like they were exercising and she was sipping water.

"Okay, I'll tell you. You ready?"

"Yeah." Arno sat back and crossed his legs. He really missed hanging out with his friends. He was looking forward to a splash fight in the Floods' indoor pool. Or a roman candle massacre in the English garden. He'd have to remember to get the gardener to give them some fireworks when they got there.

"Are you listening?"

"Yeah, yeah." He looked at her. She was smiling, like she'd thought of something really brilliant to say.

"Okay, you ready?"

"Yes, Liesel, come on, what is it?"

"We look really cool together! Isn't that enough?"

Liesel stood up. She yanked off her tiny black top and threw it at Arno. She was wearing a white silk bra studded with what looked like rubies.

She threw herself across the table, into his arms.

"Don't think about it," Liesel said. "Just, um—well . . . okay, think about it for a sec."

Arno tried to smile. If he just kind of clouded his brain a lot, he could see how they were perfect for each other, even though they couldn't agree on who the vice president of the United States was, or where Canada is.

"Maybe you're right." Arno knew his voice was

weak. He wondered where the hell Jonathan was, because he needed someone to talk some sense into him like only Jonathan could.

"Eew!"

"What?" Arno asked.

"Look at that really hairy guy! He looks like Bigfoot!"

"Where?"

Arno looked around. Liesel was pointing at a busboy. But he wasn't Bigfoot. He just had a beard.

"Hair like that freaks me out! I feel like he's going to crawl all over my body and do disgusting things!"

"Let's get you out of here."

"Okay, you want to go back to my house? My parents are in Bermuda with Governor Bloomberg for the weekend."

"He's the mayor."

"Whatever."

They began to walk through the club. The busboys and just about all of the rest of the waitstaff glared at Liesel. It occurred to Arno that, among other things, Liesel was kind of a pig.

"I'm definitely going to break up with you, the moment we get a cab," Arno said.

"What? Arno, I can't concentrate on you right now. I need to make sure that Sasquatch doesn't touch me.

And I have to pee but now I only like to go in my house—we just had new toilets installed. I love them. They're the only ones that get me truly clean."

"I'll break up with you again right when we get out on the street," Arno said. "I'm glad we spent this extra time together so we could be absolutely sure we're doing the right thing."

**why would my happiness grate on the group?**

The four of us were together in Patch's room, passing blankets and pillows back and forth, trying to get comfortable. Arno had taken the cleanest bed, and Mickey snagged the other one.

"Here, you take the beanbag chair," David said. "I'm good with the floor." I raised an eyebrow at David. Then I shrugged and took the chair.

"It's so good to see you guys," I said. "And since we're all together, I have an announcement to make." I tried to perch in the beanbag chair, which of course was impossible, so I fell backwards, which forced me to stand up.

It was strange, but I could feel everyone stiffen a little.

"I'm finally on the same wavelength as the rest of you. I am completely, totally, in love."

Mickey started laughing first.

"Actually, as of tonight, I'm definitely,

absolutely single," Mickey said.

"Me too. I'm as single as I've ever been since fourth grade," Arno said.

The three of them turned to David.

"Me too," David shrugged. He was trying to get comfortable in a corner of the room, where Patch had thrown some skiing stuff from the winter before. "I'm taking some time off from girls, just like you told me to. Remember?"

And that's when I remembered about Amanda and Froggy. David looked so depressed he must've discovered it himself, and I was thankful that I didn't have to be the one to tell him.

"So I'm the only one with a girlfriend?"

Everyone nodded.

"It's nice that you at least shared that you have a girlfriend with us. Now there's this other thing we've been wondering about," Mickey began.

But I sort of shook my head, like *no, there is no other thing.* Of course there were two other huge things—I still had to choose which friend was coming, and my dad had stolen my friends' families' money.

"I'm practically falling asleep here," I said. "I don't want to talk anymore."

"But—"

"Dude, some other time," I said. And I molded myself into the beanbag chair and closed my eyes.

"Okay," I heard Arno say, and he sounded angry. "But I'm going to say one thing. Tomorrow we're going to Greenwich, but by the time we get back, I think you should tell us who you're bringing to the Caribbean. That's what we all thought you were going to announce just now, and we think it's about time."

I heard a "yeah" and an "amen" from David and Mickey and I nodded once. "Okay. I guess that's fair," I said.

Everybody was quiet. Nobody talked about how we hadn't had a straight-up sleepover like this since we were in middle school. I lay with my eyes closed in what I hoped was the dark. I'd thought possibly being in love with Ruth was going to sail me through this weird thing that was happening with my dad, but of course I was wrong.

Then there was a crash, as a snowboard fell where it'd been leaning. It had landed on David and I could hear him wrestling with it.

# a sunny saturday in old greenwich

"Holy shit! Slow down!" David screamed. "You're going to kill us all."

"Shut up you little bitch," February Flood laughed. "You're the one who called shotgun."

Then she reached across the front seat and grabbed David's hood and yanked it over his head, just like she'd been doing since she was nine and he was five years old.

"You're looking pretty hot now that you're single, you know that David? Maybe we can get it on."

"Cut it out." David pulled the hood farther down over his stiff hair.

February snickered and turned up her Liars CD. She was best friends with Jane from the band and she sang along with herself, because she was in the background on the track.

They were blasting up the Merritt Parkway, doing ninety in her dad's canary yellow Mercedes 380SL convertible. The car was an '85, with a reconditioned engine originally built for a cargo airplane, and it could haul ass.

Arno, Mickey, and Jonathan were in the back seat, gritting their teeth. They were slowly getting their eyebrows blown off by the speed and by February's willingness to accelerate through the Merritt's frightening twists and turns.

"This isn't relaxing," Jonathan muttered, to himself.

"You all better pray that Patch shows up at the house while we're there," February said. "My parents have been at encounter sessions all week with Mr. Cult Leader Grobart about how to keep track of their son. He was the one who suggested that you all come up this weekend."

"The puppet master," Arno said.

"I heard that," David said, from the front seat.

"So what? Your dad is wacked out!"

"So is yours!" David said. "Just ask Jonathan—I bet he could tell us some stories about staying at your house!"

Everyone turned then, to look at Jonathan. This was unfortunate, because February turned too, and steered them into the breakdown lane, which had recently been graded.

The car rocked and Jonathan could only say, "Gu-gu-gu-gu-gu-gu . . ."

February got them back on the road and cut off a

few limousines and chauffeured SUVs.

"I think I bit my tongue," Jonathan said.

"Tough shit," everybody in the back seat said.

"Screw it," February said. "I think it'd probably be more effective for each of you to prove to Jonathan why you're the guy he should take on his dad's honeymoon, rather than just acting all pissy at him for inviting too many of you."

Arno said, "You know Feb, you have this amazing quality—"

"Of saying exactly what needs to be said?" February asked. "No kidding! Somebody's got to do it and you four stooges certainly don't seem up to the job."

She shot into the fast lane and gave a state trooper "the can opener," where she used one hand to wind down the fingers around her middle finger, while David grabbed the wheel.

She winked and the trooper winked back and she kept going at ninety, blowing by the Round Hill Road exit, so they had to spend twenty minutes backtracking to the Floods' estate.

"Freaking pigs," she said.

## i take a moment to enjoy flan flood's sweet lap of luxury

Even though we'd all been trotted off to the Floods' place in Greenwich since we were about eight, when we pulled off the access road, drove down the quarter mile path lined with evergreen trees on both sides, and came up to the circular driveway, I was still awed.

The thing about the Floods that I always forgot was that they had a *ton* of money. The house was four stories high and had a middle section and two gigantic wings. What it reminded me of more than anything was when you see one of those VH1 or MTV shows where they have, like, Keith Richards or one of the old guys from Pink Floyd on their estate in England and they're driving around on a golf cart in front of this huge mansion, talking about shooting pheasant. That's what it was like.

It was around two on Saturday when February

shot the Mercedes into the six car garage. She got out, slammed the door, and immediately disappeared.

"I got Patch's bedroom," Mickey said, and raced off. The rest of us shook our heads. The Flood kids had the whole west wing of the house, and there were at least five bedrooms over there, so we all ended up sleeping wherever we wanted. So while it made sense to call Patch's, since it was the best bedroom, it didn't really matter. Between now and bedtime, it was anybody's guess where we were going to end up. The only thing that was for sure was that we wouldn't see the grown-up Floods. Frederick would be puttering away at his projects at his studio-on-stilts in a cleared wood about a quarter mile from the house. And Fiona would be at the club, exercising or swimming in the indoor pool, even though they had a perfectly good workout room and a big indoor pool connected to the house.

Arno and Mickey immediately headed toward the kitchen. There was a staff here, and they always kept the place stocked with tons of stuff for heros. Mickey and Arno only had ultra-gourmet food at their houses, so they liked to fill up on bologna and salami and American cheese whenever we came to Greenwich. I heard David call from the kitchen, "Want a sandwich, dude?"

"Nah, but, um, thanks." Weird. That was so un-David.

"Hey."

I looked up. Flan Flood. Nobody'd said anything about her being here. She was, as was typical lately, in her riding outfit. There was a deep-green grass smear on the side of her thigh.

"You wipe out?"

"Yeah. Sancho bucked me."

"Does it hurt?"

She didn't answer immediately. Instead, she opened the door to the house, and I followed her in. She seemed to know that the guys were in the kitchen, so she headed toward the great room in the middle of the house, which got used officially four times a year, during benefits that the Floods threw for their favorite charities. We used it far more often—we liked to party in there. The room was about as big as a hockey rink, and the walls were all brown wood, and there were five different areas for sitting. There was a grand piano in one corner and fifty feet of glass doors that opened onto a stone patio. And beyond that were the English gardens. I know they're English because they're all very well organized and once when I was high Fiona gave me a lecture on them while everybody else raided the fridge.

Flan threw herself down on a dark leather couch and sighed.

"I miss you, Jonathan."

As usual when I was with Flan, I had one thought. She's adorable and awesome and I really like her but she's in *eighth grade*. But this time, I had something to add: *Whatever. I'm really into someone else.*

I sat down across from her on a zebra-striped chair that was actually made of zebra.

"Well. I've missed you, too. Ever since we didn't get together—I mean, it was such a surprise—and, well, I'm glad you're with Adam now." I pulled at the collar of a new Lacoste polo shirt that I'd picked up because it definitely seemed like the kind of thing you were supposed to wear on a yacht.

"Are you?"

"Everyone says he's cool."

Flan curled up on the couch. There was a big brown cashmere blanket thrown over the back and she wrapped herself up in it.

"He's okay."

"He's like the only freshman everybody knows about—there's one every year, and he's it."

"I guess. You know, Jonathan . . ."

"What?"

I had on new Tods loafers that were orange and I was still figuring out if I liked them. Lately I'd been buying so much colorful stuff I was starting to think that I might O.D. on color by the time this trip actually came around, and then I'd be by the gorgeous turquoise Caribbean water and not even appreciate it. I made a mental note to buy some more white things.

"It's warmer outside than it is in here. I'm cold. Come and sit next to me."

So just like that, I did. She was cold. I got right up next to her and rubbed her shoulders through the blanket.

"I'm still pissed at you for not going out with me," Flan said.

Then her arms were around me. She was easily as big as me, if not bigger. And she kissed me. And I let her. And of course it was incredible and something I had known I wanted to do with her for a long, long time. The thing about Flan was that she tasted sweet, just like she always seemed, and I kind of felt like if I didn't stop right then I'd never stop kissing her because it was just so nice.

"Um, this doesn't feel right," I finally said. As gently as I could, I pulled us apart.

"Why not?" She'd dug her hand under my shirt and was rubbing my chest. I glanced around the room. There were so many entrances and exits—more than I could count.

"What about you and Adam?"

"He's not here. You are."

"But you two are going out. I mean, I think you should stay with Adam."

"I don't want to." Her voice was like a warm wind. "I want to fool around with you."

"You're growing up too fast, Flan." I knew the moment the words came out that I'd pissed her off. Her eyes changed colors, from blue-green to green-black. "Look Flan, on any other weekend I'd be jumping all over you like, I dunno—the *New York Times* on last year's trend. But I'm going through something heavy right now."

"The stuff about your dad, right?"

"Yeah."

"You know, so what? Every grown-up I know seems like they do some really bad stuff, and I don't think it's such a big deal what your dad did."

I tried to smile, but it was hard, because it was *too* a big deal. Her perspective was just limited because, even though she had a big family, she was basically alone all the time, knocking around in overpriced real estate, trying to keep herself entertained, or centered, or something.

Because I wasn't saying anything, Flan stood up. There were some fresh flowers in a marble vase in the middle of the room. She walked over there—it was about half a city block—and rearranged them. When I could see she wasn't coming back, I followed her.

"Look Flan, the truth is I'm worried like crazy about it, but nobody's *saying* anything. And they're acting kind of pissed about this trip and putting all this pressure on me to decide who I'm going to bring, but I think maybe it's about more than that. David knows everything, but you're the only one I've told. You and Ruth."

"Who's Ruth?"

I stared at Flan. It was now or later, and later might be never, and I'd gotten in enough trouble with that tactic already in the last week.

"She's my girlfriend."

"Why didn't you tell me you had a girlfriend!"

She turned around quickly, grabbed some roses and threw them at my chest, then ran from the room. I shook my head. I picked up the roses and the thorns pricked my palm. There were little beads of blood there, of course.

## who goes sailing in november?

Around three or so, Arno and Mickey found me up in the common room that the Flood kids shared, which was similar to the one they shared in the city except a whole lot bigger and even more full of sports equipment. But, because the staff here was in the house more often than the Floods were, it was all very well arranged. I found it relaxing and I was leafing through an old copy of *Charlie and the Chocolate Factory* that someone had left under the cushion of a chair.

"Hey." Mickey was swaying and clearly a little wrecked. He must've eaten a lot, and drunk more. "Let's go sailing."

"Aye aye, Captain Drunky."

"I'm going to show you exactly why you should bring me on this trip."

"Dude . . ." But I could see it was to late to reason with Mickey and he was about to begin a forced-fun rampage.

"I'll drive down there," Arno said. "Because I can drive anything, like even in a place where they drive on the wrong side of the road, like St. Thomas or St. John."

David wandered into the room. He was carrying a basketball and looked a bit sweaty, so we knew he must've been playing basketball on the indoor court that the Floods had down in the old gymnasium, a couple of hundred yards from the house.

"What's up?" David began to spin the ball on one finger. Mickey tossed him a beer and he caught it and drank from it, still spinning the basketball.

"Sailing," I said.

"Uh-oh." David lost control of the ball. Neither of us had ever been any good at sailing, which of course made this honeymoon thing more than a little ironic.

We got into one of the Mercedes and Arno drove us the quarter mile down to the cove where the Floods kept their boat. This was definitely private land, since we were weaving all over the road and nobody stopped us, but there was always this sense that other super-rich types were lurking around. At least six other sailboats bobbed from moorings in the cove, and there was one old guy, in stained red pants and a yellow slicker, dousing his boat with water.

It was strangely warm out, which was one good thing. Only Mickey was shivering, since he was apparently determined to go through the fall without putting on long pants. Arno and I had put on khakis and button-downs so we were okay. David was fine too, since he immediately put his hood over his head and he was wearing a pair of those Carhartt workpants that can stop a bullet.

Immediately, Arno and Mickey clambered aboard *The Oldest Profession*, the Flood family's yacht. The thing was big, and it was bone-white with mahogany details. It looked clean and well cared for, and more expensive than a space capsule. I eyed it, figuring it was less than fifty feet long, which suddenly put this whole two-hundred-and-fifty-foot yacht thing in perspective.

"Come on," they yelled.

Mickey, who's dad had crashed more than a few sailboats out at Montauk, immediately disappeared below and came up with a bunch of yellow life preservers and several six-packs of Heineken. He threw a beer at me. "Think of me as the party guy. You can always count on me make a boat ride fun." He wagged his eyebrows at me.

"Key's in the ignition," Arno yelled. "Let's motor out of the cove." He leaped onto the dock and unfurled the ropes that were keeping the big boat steady.

I said, "I feel like this is very stupid," but mostly I was speaking to myself. The boat began to rock back and forth. Suddenly I wasn't so sure about this or any other boat, no matter how big.

"Remember what happened last time," David said as he leaped back on board.

"When Jonathan got too high," Mickey snickered. As I jumped on, I thought back on last time, when I'd done mushrooms and run around the boat for our whole trip, making sure everyone was safe and wearing life preservers and repeatedly calling the coast guard to check on the weather.

But we were already motoring out of the tiny cove, with Mickey clambering around the fore or bow or front of the boat like he was Lord Jim's apprentice and Arno behind the wheel, both of them trying to look more comfortable on the boat than I suspected they actually were. David and sat I tight. Our families weren't sailing types.

And then, when we got to the bay and we could see the Long Island Sound in the distance,

Mickey unfurled the huge sail. The wind was definitely strong and it was cooler out there.

"Drag the jib," he screamed, and, "Hazard the wickets!" Or at least that's what it sounded like. The light was incredible, low and strong and right in our eyes so we were squinting since we'd all spaced bringing sunglasses. People in other boats waved at us and we waved back and for a moment I believed we basically knew what we were doing. I won't say I felt relaxed because I didn't at all. But I did sit down to watch Arno and Mickey act like show-offs, which I knew was for my sake and I'd be lying if I said I wasn't sort of enjoying it.

We shot out to the middle of the bay, "doing a good clip," if that's what going a little too fast is called. And that's when Mickey got out some pot. He clambered down below and smoked up, and passed around what he had, which was a gigantic joint. I felt what can only be described as peer pressure so I smoked, too. I thought maybe it would calm me down and not make me start counting life preservers like last time. So I sat back and tried to feel the wind in my hair and the sun through my eyelids and tried to override the paranoia I sometimes get when I smoke with some other feeling, of trusting these guys, and getting comfortable with the feeling of water all around me. I opened my eyes.

"Careful!" I screamed.

We blew by a little fishing boat and it rocked in our wake. All the old fishermen on it gave us the finger. I felt bad for them and their families and how they weren't going to eat any fish tonight and they'd have Corn Flakes instead and it was all because of us . . . if they were fishermen. Maybe they were cops? Or marine patrol. I felt afraid for us, and bad in general for all the sins of humanity.

"Jonathan? We want to talk to you."

Arno was standing in front of me, and Mickey and David were on either side of him.

"Wha—?" I scrambled over the white seat cushions and toward the back of the boat. But of course, beyond the seats and the little wooden step we used to use to dive off, there was nothing at all. Nothing but cold water.

"There's some stuff we can't figure out," Arno said.

"Yeah," I said. "I know. I have to make some decisions."

"It's not just that," said Mickey.

This was it. I felt the paranoia leave, replaced by a terrible, frigid, reality. *My friends know everything and they are going to kill me and bury me at sea.*

"Let's not do this here," David said. "It's going to get cold soon."

"There's an island." Mickey pointed to one of those little islands that just looks like a bunch of trees growing together in a clump.

"Let's check it out," Mickey said.

I figured that they were going to take me to the island and kill me there. *My best friends are going to kill me and bury me on an island because of the sins of my father.*

"Let's just go home instead," I said quickly. I was too desperate though, and they could feel it.

"No, let's go to the island. This will be fun." Arno smiled, and wound one of the ropes around his arm. Of all of us, he could definitely sound the most menacing.

"No."

"Yes."

"Please," I said. "You can't blame me for what my dad did."

Mickey scratched his head. He'd climbed as far up the main mast he could, but he wasn't looking around—instead he was looking directly down at me.

"What did he do?" he asked. "And why haven't you told us about it?"

"I'm confused too," Arno said.

"Jonathan doesn't have to tell us everything about his life," David said.

"I think he kind of does," Arno said. "We tell him everything about our lives."

"That's true," David nodded.

"What are you going to use?" I asked.

"What?" Mickey clambered down from the mast.

"To kill me?" I was backed up against the fore or aft—the back of the boat, whatever it's called.

"What? We just want—" Arno came forward. He had a big hook at the end of a length of rope. *Dragged through the water by a hook till I tell them everything and it still won't be enough.*

It was too much. I closed my eyes and flipped over the rail. When I came up out of the water, I heard screaming, and the guys were desperately trying to turn the boat around. I bobbed along and though I felt frightened of being really cold and wet, I knew that I was at least alive. And then I guess the cold water knocked off the stupid

248

high-on-pot feeling and I realized how pointlessly paranoid I was being—*they are my friends!* And *wow*, the water was so, so much colder than the air.

The more they worked at getting back to me the farther away I got. And then I was around the tip of the island, and I was floating and cold. I started to wave at the few other boats that passed by. Minutes passed and I tried to recall what I knew about hypothermia, which was very little. And that's when I saw him.

"Patch!" I yelled. It was the oddest thing. There was Patch, on a sailboat, with Selina Trieff.

"Patch!" I thrashed around and screamed and finally, finally, I got his attention. Patch looked around, and then, after about five times as long as it'd take a normal person to recognize his best friend, he saw me.

"Hey, Jonathan," Patch called out. "You're in the water."

I watched him turn and talk to Selina, who had on gigantic sunglasses and a big piece of something white tied up in her hair. She looked beautiful. They kissed, and then Patch jumped into the water and swam over to me.

"Wow, it's freezing!" he said, and laughed. "I

saw the boat a minute ago—why aren't you on it?"

"Where is it?"

Patch pointed and then we swam around the tiny horn of the island to where the guys had managed to make *The Oldest Profession* stay still. We clambered up the ladder in the back.

"Do you guys even have a clue what you're doing?" Patch asked. David threw towels around us and we dried off as fast as we could. Luckily, it was still sunny.

Meanwhile, Patch started barking orders, and Arno and Mickey kind of skulked around looking a little embarrassed that they hadn't been such expert sailors after all. David was supposed to hold the jib, and Arno had to put his weight on the left side, and Mickey was supposed to do some other thing.

"This isn't fun," David said to me. Patch was making David sit exactly in the back middle of the boat. He wasn't supposed to move except to duck his head when the sail swung by. "You know, maybe you should take one of the other guys on the trip. I'm not sure I'm up for it anyway."

But I could tell he didn't entirely mean that. "The ring-buying's off, I take it?"

"That's for damn sure." David nodded to himself.

"Where's Selina going to go?" I asked. Patch was down to his boxers even though it was really cold, and he was scampering around fixing all the stuff we'd messed up.

"Home?"

"Oh," I said. And when I looked up, beautiful Selina Trieff was sailing away. I had a dim recollection that she had a house in Oyster Bay. She waved at us, and she looked kind of sad. I wondered how long they'd been on the boat, and whether they were going out or had slept together, or anything really. Because, since I was now with Ruth, it'd be nice to have at least one of us going out with some girl so we could maybe do stuff together once we all got back to the city. And Patch was my friend, and so were the rest of these guys, and I hoped that once we got through this weird stuff with my family we could all hang out again and things would be just like they were before.

"What an amazing girlfriend," I said.

"Girlfriend?" Patch was busy with some rope we'd ignored.

"That explains why we were having such

trouble with the boom," Mickey said.

"You guys were about to really screw up this boat," Patch said. So then I didn't ask him any more questions about Selina.

"We were going to go to that island over there." Arno pointed.

"Why?" Patch asked.

"Because," Arno looked back at David and Mickey, who were looking away. "You've missed so much of what's gong on."

Patch scratched his chin and stared at the little stand of scrub trees in the middle of the sound.

"I don't get it. So why aren't we talking about it? And why was Jonathan swimming around? Anyway, you'd destroy this boat if you got it anywhere near there. No, let's take her home. I should probably say what's up to my mom. Is she around?"

"Yeah, I think so," Arno nodded.

I sat back against the cushions on the back of the boat and sipped slowly on a beer. Everybody kept glancing at me, but now that Patch was around, nobody said anything.

"I think somebody just gave us back our moral center," David said, and he sounded all solemn, so Mickey slapped him on the back of the neck.

"I kept telling Selina that somebody was likely to get hurt if I left you guys alone for too long," Patch muttered. I heard him, and my eyes widened. And I could see that everyone else's did, too. It had never occurred to me that we needed Patch. We liked to look for him, sure, but needing him was something totally different. And suddenly I felt a little better, a little safer and a tiny bit more relaxed.

"It's too quiet—somebody put on some music," Patch said. "You guys are being weird."

Mickey scurried below to skim through Patch's dad's old Rolling Stones and Grateful Dead tapes. Next thing we knew we were listening to "Sympathy for the Devil." And Arno stuck his tongue out at me, which I definitely considered not very mature.

## david helps the guys through the heart of saturday night

Patch drove the Mercedes into the garage and everyone got out, stretched, and shivered. It was nearly dark out, and getting colder by the minute.

"I'm up for some hot chocolate," Patch said, as he opened the door. David smiled. That was the good thing about Patch. The only thought in his head was that he'd been out on a boat and now he was cold, so hot chocolate would taste good and definitely warm him up.

The door opened as they all shuffled toward it, and Flan stood there.

"You've come back," Flan said, and threw herself at the feet of her brother. She was in her riding outfit, as usual, and her helmet fell off and rolled into some bushes.

"Please," Patch said, and he tried to drag her up. Flan was definitely getting into big emotional gestures like that. It was embarrassing to watch. Flan moaned, and then kept talking, "If Mom or Dad were around, they'd be devastatingly happy to know you're alive. We could call them on their cell phones, but they've forgotten to give us the new numbers."

"Oh well," Patch said. "I'm sure they'll call to check in with you."

"Not likely." Flan laughed. She punched Jonathan in the arm and he almost fell over.

"Sorry," Flan said. "I'm going riding. See you all later." And she found her helmet and was gone.

David hung back while everyone raided the kitchen.

"I'm not that hungry," Jonathan said, to no one in particular. He got out of a jar of gherkins and found a can of Sprite and began to eat at one corner of the kitchen island. He was happy that Patch was back, and something about that made him feel weirdly centered, but he also missed the short-lived fun of having his friends compete for his attention.

Mickey veered off to the stereo and put on a Ghostface CD, loud.

"Eating-music!" Mickey said, and set out to heat up some frozen churros that had been Fed Ex'd all the way from a particularly great churro stand Frederick Flood loved in downtown L.A.

Meanwhile, Patch stood in the middle of it all. He methodically made himself a hero sandwich with roast beef, muenster cheese, assorted vegetables, coleslaw, and pieces of leftover cornish hen.

"Dude, that is so gross," David said to Patch.

Patch looked up. "You want half?"

"Yeah." David slid his plate over.

Meanwhile Arno and Mickey began to argue about what they should put on their churros to spice them up.

"You okay?" David asked Jonathan, who looked a little green around the gills from eating all those gherkins.

"I just want to go home, but of course that's impossible." Jonathan rubbed his belly and took a sip of Sprite, which appeared to make him feel no better.

"I'm sorry," David said, with his mouth full of Patch's sandwich. "I know how you feel. But we've been coming here since we were eight. It's like our second home. Isn't that enough?"

"I guess."

Once they'd stuffed themselves, they wandered into Frederick Flood's study and watched some of his porn movies from the fifties, where all of the women were really fat and laughed a lot, and the men were short, bald, and had moustaches. Then they passed out on the leather couches and napped.

When they awoke it was around ten at night, and

everyone was in a different mood. David watched the group and the only person who still seemed the least bit hyper was Jonathan. He kept standing up and walking around the library.

"Let's go hang out in the great room," Jonathan suggested. So everyone did, because there was no reason not to. Mickey went to get beers and change the music to Deathcan March.

They all settled in on the big couches that surrounded the main fireplace, which you could literally walk into without stooping. Patch went and got some big logs and built a roaring fire with flames that were several feet high.

"We could make s'mores," Patch said.

"Where's the stuff?" Mickey asked.

"What stuff?"

"The chocolate and the graham crackers and all that crap."

Patch poked at the fire. He said, "I'll tell you as soon as everyone clues me in about why Jonathan was thrashing around in the cold Sound when the rest of you were on the warm boat."

The music stopped for a moment while the system switched CDs. The gigantic logs crackled and popped, and nobody said anything. Finally, Jonathan stood up. He said, "It's been a weird week. My dad, well—my dad is getting remarried."

"Right, we all know that. *That's* what all this is about?" Patch asked.

Jonathan stared back at him. "Nah, there's more."

"Okay. So what is it?" Patch asked. "If any one of us had something bad happen, we'd be on our cellies to you in like two seconds flat. You know that."

"This is different," Jonathan said.

"In addition to being a total snob, Liesel wanted me to have a threesome with another guy," Arno said suddenly. Everyone straightened up. "See?" Arno asked. "I can tell you that."

"You broke up with her because you wouldn't do that?" Mickey asked.

"No, it was because she was arrogant, though I wouldn't've done the threesome either. Unless you were the other guy, Mickey." Arno threw himself back among the pillows.

"I don't think Liesel liked me enough to fool around with me," Mickey said.

"Oh, stop. What about you? Tell us a secret," Arno said to Mickey.

"Philippa and I," but Mickey stopped. He looked as if he were choking on something.

"What is it?" Arno asked. He tossed a bottle of Corona over to Mickey who just caught it and narrowly missed knocking over a marble bust of Eleanor Roosevelt that stood on a pedestal next to where he was sprawled out.

"I think the truth is that we broke up because we're so in love that we can hardly look at each other. And I was always disappointing her. I'm just too wild . . . though I don't feel particularly wild right now."

Everyone was quiet for a moment. In the background, Mr. Flood's old *Morrison Hotel* album made the dark room even spookier.

"That's ridiculous," David said. "Nobody ever—"

But Arno was pointing to David and sort of bouncing up and down, which was unusual for him since he usually kept his cool no matter what.

"Bullshit!" Arno said. "You and Amanda started cheating on each other for the same kind of dumb reason."

"Kind of." David frowned. "I only started up with Risa to get back at Amanda."

"Dude," Mickey said. "That's terrible."

"And now Amanda is fooling around with—" David stopped.

"Don't say it," Jonathan said.

"Froggy." David moaned. "I walked in on them last night. And it's all because she wanted to get engaged so we'd stop cheating on each other, and I knew that was a weird artificial thing and the truth is that she's too insecure for me to handle."

"That's got to be fixable," Jonathan said.

"Well, when you figure out how, let me know."

"Wow." Patch had his feet curled up under him like a little kid. He'd managed to balance his beer bottle on a pillow, but now when he spoke, the bottle flipped over and poured down the front of the couch. Jonathan caught it, but he was a little late. Patch immediately took off his shirt and wiped up the spill. "You guys are like—there's a reason I'm still best friends with you guys. You're so honest with each other. I mean it's amazing that we're capable of this kind of thing. It's really cool."

Arno saw Jonathan looking gratefully at Patch. But he didn't get why.

"What about you and Selina Trieff?" Arno asked, quickly. He knew the attention was supposed to be on Jonathan and his problem, but all the stuff that was coming out was too interesting to be ignored. "Did you two not just spend the last three days on her sailboat?"

"Yeah. She's really fun."

"That's it?" David stood up, walked the fifty feet to the electronics cabinet and changed the music to the new Flaming Lips CD. "We reveal all this stuff and you say that Selina Trieff is 'fun'?"

For a moment, everyone stared at Patch. But Arno turned and looked at Jonathan, who had his eyes closed as if he were praying.

"Well I don't know how to say too much more about her than that. So you guys threw Jonathan in the sound because his dad is getting remarried? Which, hello, we already knew."

"No. I landed in the water because my dad invited me on his honeymoon which will be on this huge sail-boat in the Caribbean that my dad's new wife PISS owns and the thing is, I was only allowed to invite one of you, but I invited all of you. Except for you, Patch, and that's just because I couldn't find you," Jonathan said. Everybody was quiet then, watching.

"Um," Patch said. "Okay. That doesn't seem like such a big deal though, right? I mean, you'll take some-one and, whatever, maybe the rest of us will meet up with you in Harbour Island anyway or something."

David smiled and said, "That's a good idea." Then he added, "But we didn't throw him in the sound."

"Yeah," Jonathan said. "Anyway, it's not just that. There's this other thing—"

"That you won't tell us about," Mickey said.

"If I told you guys about it," Jonathan said. "I'd have to like, beg you all for forgiveness."

"So? We'd give it to you," Arno said.

"I don't think I'm ready yet," Jonathan said. He folded his arms and looked out the window. David followed his glance. There was nothing but trees and darkness out there. David settled himself into his seat and thought about how he knew what Jonathan's father did, and Mickey half-knew, but Arno and Patch totally didn't. It was a mess.

"Didn't we just talk about our girlfriends?" Mickey asked.

"*This is bigger than that,*" Jonathan whispered. Everyone was quiet.

"Maybe we shouldn't do this right now," Patch said. "Not if Jonathan's not ready."

Everyone stared at him. He wanted to say that he'd never heard Patch say anything definitive before, but he knew that wouldn't be cool.

"Maybe you should all sleep on it," Flan Flood said, from the door. And of course nobody knew how long she'd been standing there. That made everyone uncomfortable enough to head up to bed.

## mickey should never be allowed to drive anything

On Sunday, February Flood was nowhere to be found and everyone had to get back to the city. The five of them discussed this while sitting in the great room, where they'd carried their breakfasts on big white plates.

"At least we found you, Patch," Arno said. "Mission accomplished. Your parents are going to be psyched." He balanced his plate on one knee—they'd cooked everything they could find, so each of them had about five eggs and half a pound of bacon on their plates.

"I'm sorry I couldn't tell you guys more stuff," Jonathan said, and to Mickey, he sounded like he meant it.

"Let's lay off him," Mickey said. "He's our friend."

"Still." Arno went back to stuffing himself. "I don't even get what he's hiding. What could be so bad? Take my family for example. I bet my parents cheat on each other all the time."

And then Mickey got up and ran over to Arno and

put him in a headlock, and what was left of Arno's food spilled onto the rug.

"It's just like when we were in fifth grade," David said quickly.

"If it were like back then," Mickey gasped, as he held Arno down and gently banged his head against the floorboards, "I'd be kicking *your* ass too."

"All that pot has ruined your memory," David said, and laughed. And Mickey had to laugh too, because he knew as well as anyone that even though David was a mope, he was physically bigger and in much better shape because of basketball, and thus could kick everyone's asses. Then and now.

A few hours later, when everyone was ready to go, they went looking for Patch. He was out in the back garden. He'd come across a dove that was cooing from the branches of an old spruce tree, and he ended up sitting at the foot of the tree and cooing up at it. Clearly the bird was psyched, because it was now on Patch's shoulder and appeared to be pecking lightly at Patch's lips. As usual, everyone stared in wonder at Patch.

"I'm sure they called," Patch said, to no one in particular, when they found him.

"Are you talking about your parents?" Mickey asked.

"Well, yeah."

"I talked to my parents and they said they ran into

them at the airport," Mickey said as he clambered up into the spruce tree. "They're headed to Switzerland for the week."

"Oh, okay," Patch said. "Let's take Big Bird and go home."

"What's he talking about?" Arno asked.

"The yellow car we came up in," Mickey said. "He's going to let me drive."

"Who said?" Patch asked.

"Um." Mickey frowned. No one had said. And everybody knew that.

The boys packed their stuff and got out of the house after Patch left a handwritten note for the staff, saying that they were going. Because it was Sunday, they weren't around. And the house was in pretty bad shape.

"At least we didn't burn anything down," Jonathan said as they pulled out of the driveway, with Patch driving. They all looked back at the house. Once when they were eleven, they built a fort in the woods and Mickey pretended to be an American Indian. He lit the fort on fire and the fire department had to be called to put out the trees. After that, Mickey was banned from the Floods' estate for six months, and his dad had to give the Floods a piece of sculpture. It still stood in the back-yard and was now worth three quarters of a million dol-lars. The sculpture was supposed to have been an abstraction, but everyone could see that it kind of looked like an Indian setting a white man's ass on fire.

Patch took the wheel and drove fast down the path of rolling hills that led them out of the Flood estate and out to the highway. In the backseat, David and Arno seemed to be asleep. Jonathan sat squished between them, on the hump. Jonathan leaned forward so his head was between Mickey's and Patch's.

"You know, you're kind of the most capable of any of us even though you're sort of the biggest blow-off," Jonathan said, to Patch.

"Shhh," Mickey said. "Don't hurt his feelings while he driving."

They shot down the Merritt in silence for a while, with Mickey mostly brooding in the front passenger seat. Patch drove faster and faster, a toothpick dangling from his mouth. He was in oversized corduroys and a black flannel shirt. His dirty blond hair was standing up and he had several days worth of stubble on his cheeks. Mickey shook his head. He pretended he didn't care about such things, but Patch sure was a hell of a lot better looking than any of the rest of them, except maybe Arno.

"Wait!" Mickey yelled. "This is Thanksgiving week! This is a short week! Oh man!"

"What's the difference?" Arno asked, with both eyes

closed. "You only go to school when you want to anyway."

"Still—this is a party week, and that's fun."

"Last week was a party week," Arno said.

"Yeah . . . but we all know what this Wednesday is," Patch said. Everyone stopped and looked at him. Even David, who had seemed pretty asleep, opened one eye.

"When did you start knowing stuff about days in the future?" Arno said. "And when'd you get your driver's license anyway?"

There was quiet for a moment. This was true. Mickey eyed Patch.

"Yeah, Patch, who are you really?" Mickey asked.

But Patch ignored them all. He said, "Wednesday is Ginger Shulman's annual pre-Thanksgiving bash."

"Where's she having it this year?" Arno asked. "Your house, again?"

"No, hers." Patch expertly swung in and out of the fast lane, passing absolutely everyone.

Then it was quiet for a while. Mickey was sure they were all chewing on the idea of the new Patch who was driving them all home. And in the back of his mind, Mickey waited for the question he knew was coming.

"Hey, Mickey?" Jonathan asked.

"Sure," Mickey nodded. "You've already stayed at everybody else's house, now you should stay at mine."

"Thanks for not making me ask."

"We're *all best friends.*" Mickey smiled. "You need to chill the fuck out."

But even as Mickey spoke, Jonathan looked away. And they both knew the truth, that Jonathan kind of *had* asked. And Mickey had the weird, uncertain feeling that Jonathan had been avoiding his house because he knew things that Mickey didn't.

The sky grew dark as they coasted into the city, and everyone seemed to sleep except Patch, who hummed along with the *Flower Power Hour* on WFMU.

They arrived at Fifth Avenue and, since everybody else lived west of there, Jonathan clambered out first.

"I'll see you at your house later," Jonathan said to Mickey.

"Cool. It's Sunday, right? There'll probably be some huge-ass dinner party. We can drink wine and pass out in front of the TV during prime time football."

Everybody waved to Jonathan as the yellow Mercedes roared off down Eleventh Street.

### i must reveal my secrets!

I breathed a deep sigh of relief. They were gone. I stood there on a corner I'd known for my entire life and leaned against the limestone of my building, which had been there since 1895. I knew I was totally afraid of them and that I really needed to either throw myself at their mercy, or lose them entirely and start fresh. And if I did that, if I lost my friends, who would I be? I had no idea. Patch had saved me from having to choose who was coming on this trip with me, but I knew that problem obviously wasn't half as important as I'd been thinking it was.

And that's when I saw the black English cab the Halstead Real Estate company uses to ferry buyers around. It pulled up in front of my apartment building, and another couple of young, rich-looking people came out of my front door, with one of those real estate ladies who wear way too much gold. They were talking in low voices and then they got into the car. I shook my head. I definitely, definitely couldn't handle both at the same time—losing my friends *and* moving to Brooklyn. It would just be too much. I had to tell them the truth. But how? Part of me wished David would just gossip it to them, since he knew. But he was too good of a friend to do that, which was something.

Before I went upstairs to see what new damage Billy the painter had done to my house, and whether it had been sold over the weekend, I called Ruth.

"Mmm." Her voice. It was smoky and very warm. "I was taking a nap."

"I can hear that. I missed you."

"You were away all weekend?"

"Yeah. I was with my guys, but right now I just want to hang out with you."

"Why didn't you call me from wherever you were?"

"Well, I felt too . . . too *guy-like* with all my friends. I wanted to wait."

"Huh. I guess that's good." I could hear her rustle in her bed, and it was so the place I'd have rather been than on the windy corner of Eleventh and Fifth with a bright street lamp shining down on me and my Ghurka weekender bag at my feet.

"You know how the thing happens where after you meet someone you start hearing about them all the time, like the person you're thinking about keeps coming up in conversation with the most random people?"

"Yeah." I braced myself.

"Everyone's talking about you and your guys. It's like the moment I leave the house or get on the phone I hear somebody mention you or one of the others of you, which only makes me think of you."

"The others of me?"

"I mean—the rest of you, the other four."

"But we're all different."

"Right. I talked to your friend Liza. It's barely Thanksgiving and you guys have already had a really wild year. I'm sort of a quiet person, Jonathan, I'm not sure I can handle how notorious you guys are."

"Look, forget everything you've heard. When can I see you?"

"I—not till Wednesday, at Ginger Shulman's party."

"Not till then?"

"Yeah, I've got a bioethics exam on Tuesday

and then my school has a homecoming luncheon on Wednesday. I'm sorry. Maybe we can meet up before the party starts."

"Let's do that. How was Harvard?" I asked.

"Harvard? Oh yeah. It was good. I'm into Harvard."

"You mean like you like it?"

"No, I'm going there."

"But you're only a junior."

"I know but the president told me it was no problem. We ended up having some sherry together in his office. He told me that so long as he was president, there was a place for me there. The administration is letting the kids have their own porn magazine this year—Harvard is definitely getting to be a really cool place." She yawned. "Mmm. Let's talk later. I miss you."

And then she got off the phone.

"When will it be over?" Richard wailed, in the elevator.

"I don't know." I knew I sounded all grave and like I was talking about so many more things than just the painting of my apartment, which I definitely was.

"I'm sorry. It's not sold yet, is it?"

"I don't know about that," Richard snuffled. "But when your mother gets home, boy, the whole building wants to have a word with her."

"Great."

Richard opened the elevator door on my floor. The smell of paint was overwhelming and Richard covered his mouth. Through his gnarled fingers, he said, "That jackass in there, not only is he painting, he's running a one-man whore-house!"

And before I could respond, Richard slammed the elevator door closed and left me there. The apartment door was open, and I slipped inside. Billy was playing Neptunes remixes, very loudly. I pulled up my shirt to cover my nose and mouth. All the windows were open and it was cold in there.

"Hello!"

Billy wandered in from the kitchen. He was wearing no shirt and the pants from my blue Paul Smith suit, which my mom had bought me just two months earlier for early college interviews. The suit had cost her two thousand dollars. Of course the pants were smeared with purple and white paint.

"Hey, I loved those pants." I sighed. "Have you

273

heard from my mom?"

"Yeah. She checked in yesterday. How are you, dude?"

"You've ruined all my clothes."

"Well they're just clothes, right?"

I didn't speak. I would've sat down, except there was nowhere to sit. Everything was covered in canvas tarps, and there was wet paint on all the tarps. I looked up. We were standing in the hallway and he'd painted a sort of spindly design all up and down the ceiling, with crazy arrows pointing to different rooms. What appeared to be lyrics from ancient Jimi Hendrix songs were written in bright green script.

"Billy," I said. "I'm in trouble. Not as much trouble as you're going to be in when my mom finds out what you've done to our house, but trouble."

"Tell me about it."

He had this weirdly open smile. I could see why my mom trusted him. I wondered if she might even decide to like his awful paint job.

"My friends want to know exactly what the hell is going on with me."

"Yeah, so tell them."

But then I remembered something, and

glanced around.

"Is my friend Mickey's mom here?"

"Lucy? No," Billy said, and smiled.

"Are you having an affair with her?"

Billy laughed. "Let's deal with your problems first, before we get into mine."

"Do you know what my father did?"

"No, but I do know that if there is a secret, you need to be able to tell your friends, otherwise they're not your friends."

"Yeah. Are you sleeping with all their moms, though?"

"What do you think of the ceiling?" Billy asked.

"I can't talk to my friends about all this. Not yet, not till my mom gets back anyway, and I find out if we're going to have to move to Brooklyn and never show my face anywhere cool again."

"Any of them know?"

"Well, David pretty much knows. Patch probably doesn't care, Arno's too self-involved to figure it out, and Mickey, well, I think Mickey half-knows. And he's going to go nuts soon, for sure. He's been way too sane lately. Plus, there's whatever you're up to with his mom."

"If you know your guys that well, I'm sure

275

you'll be able to work it out."

"What about the other thing?"

"His mom? Sounds like you've got bigger stuff to worry about."

"Hmm," I scratched my chin and watched him. Billy was whistling. Then, as if on some weird cue, the music switched to "Let It Be."

"Where did you come from, really?" I asked.

"Everybody asks me that." Billy climbed up a ladder and began to write the words to "Let It Be" on the ceiling in a pattern that seemed to lead into the hall closet. I wondered if this was some weird message: Let the mess in the hall closet be?

"If you do see Lucy Pardo, tell her I miss her," he said.

"Dude, no way."

And I wandered off to my room to try to save at least the jacket that went with those Paul Smith pants, since that suit did fit me really, really well.

**in the valley of the pardos**

"I'm only going to be here three nights and they built me a bed?" Jonathan asked. They were in Mickey's room in the Pardos' massive house on West Street.

Suspended from the ceiling by lengths of inch-thick chain was a small bed that swayed gently in the breeze from Mickey's oversized window. The bed was above their heads, and Mickey began to crank a little motor. After a moment, it began to descend slowly, and unevenly.

"Looks like something from the Spanish Inquisition," Jonathan said.

"My dad designed it just for you."

"I'm only going to be here till Wednesday night. This is like, so unnecessary."

The bed was now only a few feet from the floor. They watched it as if it were going to jump. Mickey toyed with the iPod in his pocket and adjusted the music. He was currently into a set of RZA bootlegs from 1999.

"Try it."

"I'm afraid." Jonathan reached forward and tugged on the leather blanket, then pulled back as if it were going to bite him. Then he slowly got onto the bed, and sat in the middle of it. He smiled at Mickey.

"This is pretty cool."

"Yeah," Mickey said. "Let me on there." So Mickey started to get on, and immediately the chains rattled and the bed upended itself, and both boys landed on the floor in a heap.

"Ow!" Mickey leaped up. "Caselli!"

"Yeah?" Caselli came in.

"The bed doesn't work."

"Sure it does." Caselli climbed onto the now-still bed and lay there, with his arms folded over his stomach like a mummy in a casket. "See?"

"I get it," Mickey nodded. "No sudden moves on the Inquisition-guest-bed."

Caselli got off and worked the winch, and the bed slowly ascended toward the ceiling. He said, "If you were going to like, do something that involved pleasure, this would not be the bed to do it on."

"That's fine," Jonathan said. "It's not like I'd ever come back here and sleep on it drunk or anything."

Jonathan and Mickey smiled at each other since it was a party week and that was obviously going to happen. Caselli gave them a look. Mickey wandered toward the door.

"Where are you going?" Jonathan leaped up, as if suddenly afraid to be alone in the house.

"Um, the kitchen? You want anything?"

"Oh, okay, sure. I'll have whatever you're having."

"Me and Philippa used to do tequila slammers in the kitchen after school . . ."

"Dude, I'm sorry those days are over."

"Stay here," Mickey said. "Try to figure out how you're going to sleep in that bed."

Mickey went to the kitchen and found a roast beef and some vegetables simmering on the stove. He put together a couple of plates and snagged some cans of Tecate from one of the refrigerators.

They were supposed to have Sunday dinner but when Mickey glanced up, it was already eight o'clock, so he guessed that maybe it wasn't happening. He padded slowly back to his room with the food.

When he got to his door, he heard voices and he stopped. He didn't have any kind of antenna for gossip, but something did feel off. Then he figured it out. It was his mom's perfume—he had no idea what it was called, it was just mom-smell to him—coming from his room. She was in there with Jonathan. Mickey put his ear to the wall.

"You never saw me at your house. Do you understand that?" Lucy Pardo was saying.

"Okay," Jonathan said.

"We are more than happy to provide for you here. We even built you this bed, but I need to be assured that the only place you know me from is this house, where I am Mickey's mom. Right?"

"Okay," Jonathan repeated. Mickey looked at the floorboards for a moment and tried to figure out what was going on. Just as he got ready to go into his room and ask both of them exactly that, his mom came out.

"Hi, darling." She walked past him quickly, only pausing to run a hand over his great mass of spiky hair, which he realized, in that moment, he only kept up because she liked it that way. Mickey went into his room and put the food down.

"Dude, what is the deal with you and my mom?"

Jonathan just shook his head. He seemed to be staring at a point on the ceiling. And when Mickey looked he saw that he was looking up at the bed.

"Man," Jonathan said. "I am really afraid to sleep in that thing."

Above them, the black-leather-covered bed swayed back and forth and the lengths of thick chain clanked together in a way that could only be described as

283

forbidding.

"Tell me the truth, Jonathan."

"If I had a clue, I would." Jonathan leaned against Mickey's desk. "I'm ditching school in the morning and going to Tootsi Plohound. I need a new pair of boots and I want to see if the new Prada flip-flops are cool or not. You want to come?"

"I wouldn't want to go shopping even if I did understand what you were talking about." Mickey was chewing on the collar of his T-shirt, watching Jonathan.

"If my mom were doing something wrong, you'd tell me, wouldn't you?"

"Yeah." But Jonathan looked away. He said, "I'm so tense lately I can't even go to the bathroom for real."

"Well, I'll leave if you want to use mine."

"No, it's not the same as using mine at home."

"I know what you mean," Mickey said. "You do look a little heavy, like with secrets and stuff, huh?"

"Mmm," Jonathan said.

"Look dude, I'll make you a deal. You tell me what's going on before your mom gets back, okay? Before you leave here."

"And what'll you do?"

"Well, I won't kill you. And the Caribbean . . . well, it's fine. I won't go. And if there's some other bullshit that's going on with you, I promise I won't get upset about whatever it is."

"Actually, that sounds pretty fair," Jonathan said. And they sat down to eat.

## how little does homecoming matter to arno?

Arno came out of school and Mickey was standing there waiting for him. It was Wednesday, lunchtime, and everyone was being let out of school early for homecoming and the Thanksgiving holiday. Arno had been through a rough couple of days. His mom and dad didn't appear to be speaking to each other, and Mickey's dad kept calling his house. Arno had no idea why. He wanted to ask Mickey, but he doubted Mickey would know anything about what his father was up to since he avoided his father as much as he possibly could.

Arno turned up his collar and stuffed his hands into his blazer pockets. He didn't have a schoolbag with him since he didn't have any plans to do any work over the break.

"They let you all out earlier than us?" Arno asked Mickey.

"No, I'm still supposed to be there. But they were going to do all that homecoming bullshit, so I cut out."

Mickey shivered. He was in shorts, flip-flops and a white leather motorcycle jacket. The Gissing kids stared at him.

"Everything cool with Jonathan at your house?" Arno asked.

"Yeah—I've barely seen him, actually. I know he went to school the last couple of days, and then he hung out at his house with that painter. We were supposed to meet up today, though."

"What are we doing now?" Mickey asked.

"Don't we usually go to the movies?" Arno suggested.

It was true. In the past they'd cut out of homecoming activities and everything else and gone to whatever joke movie was playing—*Old School* or *Riddick* or any of that other garbage—the stupider the better. They always erred in favor of those in the group who couldn't possibly sit through a whole movie unless they were high.

"Yeah, I think *Fog of War* is playing. We can go as soon as Jonathan comes out," Arno said, nodding at the main entrance to Gissing. "David's playing Potterton's student/alumni basketball game, right? What about Patch?"

"I heard that Patch went to school today."

"Huh."

"He *went*. He didn't *arrive*."

"Right." Arno checked his watch. It was a seventies Rolex he'd snagged from his dad, and it was so big it made his wrist look feminine. With his blazer, he wore a turtleneck and jeans. "Aren't you freezing?" Arno asked.

"Kind of. Why don't we go watch David play ball. I bet there'll be girls there."

"Our exes?"

"Yeah, but more, besides." The truth was Mickey wasn't really up for seeing other girls yet, but he knew exactly how to get Arno's attention.

"All right, cool. It'll be like . . . like scouting for Ginger Shulman's party later." Arno smiled to himself at that thought.

"Hey man," Mickey threw an arm around Jonathan as he came out of Gissing. "Let's get you over to Potterton to see some good basketball and bad women."

"Okay, why not." Jonathan said.

Mickey hailed a cab.

"I talked to Ruth," Jonathan said. "She'll be at Ginger's but she can't see me till then. I can't believe I'm the only one of us with a girlfriend."

"Yeah, that is weird." Arno twisted the dial on his Rolex but the click-click-click sound faded away when the cab took off across town.

Later, Arno called Patch, which felt particularly sur-
real since it happened so rarely. Neither of them were
phone guys.

"It was cool. David got a triple double and stuffed
on that kid Alex who's playing for Yale this year.
Remember Alex? We hated that kid. And now David
stuffed his ass."

"Sounds cool," Patch said.

"I'm home," Arno said. "I'm just going to change
and shit, before we head to Ginger Shulman's, which is
at her parents' new apartment this year. I bet everybody'll be there. Definitely Liesel—I told you I blew
her off, right?"

"What's up?" Patch said. But Arno knew he wasn't
talking to him. Patch liked to buy presents for his family for Thanksgiving rather than Christmas, so he was
out shopping.

"Are you in SoHo?"

"I gotta go," Patch said. "I see Selina Trieff, or I
think I'm supposed to meet her, and she's here."

"Dude, is she your girlfriend or isn't she?"

But Patch was already gone. Arno let himself into his
house, which was bustling with strangers. There were
always workmen in there, hanging art from the gallery

or taking it down, or there were cooks preparing food for a benefit or special event his parents were having in one of the common rooms.

"Hello there, boy," his dad said. "Have you seen your mom?"

"No."

Arno and his dad stared at each other. Where was Allie Wildenburger?

"Where have you been?"

"Um, me and the guys just saw a movie. And we're meeting up again in a couple of hours."

Mr. Wildenburger's nose was twitching like a rabbit's, and the foxes on his velvet loafers seemed to be baring their teeth at Arno.

"Ask around for your mother, would you? For me? I'm off."

"To where?"

"Paris."

"But Dad, tomorrow's Thanksgiving!"

"It's also the day your friend Jonathan's father's getting married, and that's more important."

"You're his best man, yeah? Didn't you say that earlier?"

"Now I'm his worst man. I've got to get there and serve him papers before his new wife can lay claim to his money. Oh wait—"

"What?"

"You're not supposed to know any of this. You're totally confused, aren't you? Save me some turkey. I'll see you on the weekend." And with that, Mr. Wildenburger strode out of the living room.

Arno landed with a thump on the couch and wondered if this had something to do with why Jonathan had been so weird lately. But wasn't the new wife rich? What about that huge yacht and the sailing trip?

"One other thing." Arno's dad poked his head back in. "Tell your mother that if I find out she's been spending time with Ricardo Pardo, I'm going to murder them both."

"I don't know what you're talking about," Arno spoke plaintively. He couldn't figure out what Mickey's dad had to do with anything.

"Right. You shouldn't know any of this. Forget I said anything. Sorry." And Arno's dad was gone.

## david brings someone special to ginger's

David and Patch walked through Times Square. Patch preferred to walk everywhere if he could. Even though the wind was whipping their butts and it was dark and cold, Patch was in sandals, paper-thin khakis, and a torn white-linen blazer over an ancient pink oxford shirt. David, for what might have been the first time in his life, asked himself a fashion question: Was dressing with a screw-you attitude toward the weather the cool thing to do? And if so, why?

David wrapped himself tighter in the black North Face down coat his parents had bought him the weekend before.

"You know, we never hang out together alone," Patch said. They were wandering slowly up to Ginger Shulman's party at One Columbus Circle.

"Well, we're . . ." But David trailed off. He wanted to say they were about as different as two people could be, but he couldn't find the right words. Instead he said, "Do you think Selina will be there?"

Patch was quiet for a moment. Then he said, "You know, I hadn't really thought about it. I like her though, I think."

"Well, have you called her?"

"No, but we saw each other yesterday. I think we might've talked about being in love."

"You can't remember?"

"Nah." Patch looked away from David.

They kept going. David's phone vibrated against his chest. Amanda. He took the call.

"Are you going to be at the party?" she asked.

"Well, yeah. I was planning on it. Why?"

"Because then I can't go. I don't want to see you."

"Oh come on Amanda—don't be like that."

Right then, Patch tapped David on the arm. He gestured for the phone. David gave it to him.

"Hey Amanda, this is Patch . . . Yeah, I know—we've definitely never spoken on the phone before. Anyway, it'd be great if you came to the party tonight. I don't feel like I've seen you in weeks. And I'd love to be with you and David, because the two of you together are so great. So you'll come? Good. See you there." Patch handed the phone back to David.

For a minute, David was too shocked to say anything. Then he said, "Wow. First you drive, now you fix things."

"I know one problem we need to fix, and that's whatever's going on with Jonathan."

"Yeah, I think you're right about that."

"My little sister—she cares about him and she said he's all messed up. She said we're his best friends, so we've got to be there for him."

David smiled. He thought, *if only Patch were just around more, we'd all be less screwed up*. But of course the problem was just that, Patch was never around. Then they both glanced up at a forty-foot-tall photo of a lingerie model they knew from kindergarten, and David managed to grab Patch just before he stepped into traffic and disappeared for good.

## mickey's magic slammer

"Even if you totally screw it up it's still tequila and ginger ale, and that's pretty good," Liesel yelled.

Mickey nodded at her. He'd only met her a couple of times, but Arno's problem was obvious. She was really, really good-looking, but she brayed like a donkey and she said the most annoying shit.

They were in the Shulmans' kitchen and a little line had formed in front of Mickey, who was showing everyone how to do tequila slammers. It turned out that the Shulmans had a whole cabinet full of high quality tequilas—Maduros, and Mezcals, and Marinahas—and Mickey was methodically finishing each bottle. He had plenty of ice and cold ginger ale by his side and he was getting really into pouring slammers down everyone's throats. He'd arrived early for no particular reason, except of course that he'd known Ginger since a round-the-world trip they'd taken together with their parents when they were ten. Ginger's parents owned a chain of bookstores, and her dad was really, really into buying art. So he loved Mickey's dad. And of course, Mickey's dad loved him right back.

"Could somebody tell my friends I'm in here, when they get here?" Mickey asked. He brought a paper-towel-covered crystal shot glass up in the air and slammed it down on the black granite counter, then uncovered it and threw the shot down Liesel's throat. It was her fourth in a row, but nobody had the courage to push her out of line.

"Fuck me so hard!" Liesel yelled, after she caught her breath.

"I think David and Patch just got here," Adam Rickenbacher said. He was next in line and getting really annoyed at Liesel.

"What about Arno?" Mickey asked.

"Don't speak of him!" Liesel screamed. She grabbed the shot glass and flung it at Mickey, who ducked, so it sailed through the kitchen entranceway, through the formal dining room, and into the reception room, where it banged against the head of a girl named Simone, who was talking with Philippa, who'd just arrived.

"Ow!" Simone said, and fell against a gigantic Matthew Barney photograph of a satyr.

"So we broke up because we're so in love but we're just really different," Philippa said to Simone as she helped her stand up again.

"Do you really believe that?" Simone asked, while she rubbed her bruised head.

"I keep trying to. Does it sound sensible at all?"

"No. Could you get me some ice?" Simone stumbled to the couch.

Meanwhile, Mickey was backing away from Liesel, who was demanding more shots.

"Help!" Mickey ran out of the kitchen, swinging Ginger Shulman into Liesel's path. It was around eleven and the party was coming into its own. Mickey knew he was at the center of it. He could do whatever he wanted in Ginger's house. It was almost as good as Patch's house that way. And there was Patch! By the window, talking with Selina Trieff and some other stunning girls in short skirts and black tights and tall boots. David was with him, but he was off to one side with Amanda, their heads bowed in toward each other like a couple of nesting birds.

"Let's do a slammer," Mickey said to Patch once he'd gotten Liesel off him.

"A popper."

"Call it whatever you want, they're in the kitchen." Mickey grabbed Patch and David, who only fought briefly before giving in. They paraded toward the kitchen and the music got big—it was old White Stripes, *White Blood Cells*.

"Arno's on his way?" David asked.

"Yeah, and Jonathan?" Patch asked.

"Jonathan's right there," Mickey said, because Jonathan was. He was on a couch with Ruth, who Patch and Mickey hadn't even met yet. Jonathan was in a black T-shirt, jeans, and black boots. He looked, Mickey thought, tougher than he was supposed to look.

"Hey guys," Jonathan stared up at them, as they surrounded him. Neither he nor Ruth got off the couch.

"Popper?" Mickey nodded at the kitchen.

"Yeah, in a minute."

And even to Mickey, it was apparent that things were not well between Jonathan and Ruth.

"You want us to bring you out something?" David asked.

"Just give us a few minutes." Jonathan and Ruth were sitting close on the couch, but they weren't touching each other. The room was thick with people, and the music was keeping conversations loud, but it was pretty obvious that whatever they were talking about wasn't good.

The guys strode into the kitchen. Mickey pushed aside some younger guys who were doing slammers on their own, and he took over operations.

"What's the matter with Jonathan?" David asked Patch.

"The thing with Jonathan is he can get pretty emotional about things. That's why I like him, I guess." Patch accepted a foaming slammer from Mickey.

"Yeah," David said. "He's definitely emotional. We should talk with him later. Clear some stuff up about—" But before David could finish he had a slammer under his nose, and as he tried to get it down he sneezed and tequila and ginger ale went all over Selina Trieff's shirt, and she slugged him. Then David's eyes started to water and it looked like he was crying.

"This party's killer!" Mickey screamed. He leaped up on the counter and tried to slam one over his head on the ceiling. He was making a huge mess, but of course Ginger Shulman was nowhere to be found.

## the bathroom of my destiny

"I think I should go," I said to Ruth. But I didn't stand up.

Before the party we'd tried to have dinner together at Brasserie in midtown because my mom was friends with the owner, but as it turned out he was also a former client of my dad's and he wouldn't give me a table, so we ended up walking up to Ginger's in the cold. We'd been on the couch for two hours. And Ruth had taken most of that time to slowly and carefully break up with me.

"I'm sorry," she said. She still looked beautiful. She had on these stiletto highheeled boots, black pants, and a tight little Michael Stars T-shirt. She sipped at the glass of white wine she'd poured herself when we came in. She wasn't much of a drinker.

I kind of felt like I'd been listening to Ruth for too long. But her point, that I'd come on too strong and now she felt pressure from me, was a good one. I couldn't deny that. And she wanted to think about Harvard and how pretty she was and the great life she had. Of course she didn't see it that way. But I did. And me? I was thinking that if we ended the night apart, I'd be really low—as low, and this dawned on me quickly, as the low of how it feels to have a bucket of cold water dumped on you when you're at camp and sleeping naked because it's so hot and they've dragged you and your bed into a field and gotten some icy water from the kitchen and thrown it on you so you'll pee all over the place and wake up screaming. I would be as low as I'd ever been since that happened.

"I used to go to camp with Ginger," I said, because Ruth was being so quiet. "Boy did we ever play practical jokes on each other at that camp."

I stood up. My new boots were a little slick on the soles and I shimmied for a second on the slick wooden floor.

"I may not be here when you get back," Ruth said. I took her hand, suddenly, and kissed it.

I turned then, and walked toward Ginger's parents' bedroom, but then I caught a glimpse of someone who was so out of place here but some-how set me immediately at ease. Flan. She saw me, too, and she waved and smiled in a really quiet, warm way.

I sighed. I can't quite describe the feeling I was having as anything but relief. She was just who I needed to see. I started walking toward her, but then I saw that she was talking to that Adam kid, and she made a little sign with her hand that said *one minute*, and I realized it sort of looked like she was giving the same talk to Adam as Ruth had just given to me. I nodded at her and kept going toward Ginger's parents' bathroom. On the way I passed Arno, who'd just arrived. He was deep in conversation with one of Liesel's cute friends, and he barely noticed me.

It was still early enough in the night that no one was using Ginger's parents' bedroom to hook up. I strode through and went into the bath-room, where it was very quiet. Once inside, I flipped the lock and took a deep breath. The bath-room was big and new, with two sinks and a tile shower stall enclosed with thick slabs of glass. The floor was white marble, with pink and red veins running through it. Speakers embedded in the ceiling played the same music that everyone at the party was hearing, but the temperature was different in here—it was warmer, and I could feel the hushed vents pulling out the bad air and pumping in good air.

There was a new steel tub on a platform, too, and a comfortable chair in one corner, under a window. I looked out the window as I undid my belt, and saw the moon. I felt like apologizing to it. *I'm sorry I screwed up my life, or let it get screwed up, or whatever.*

I checked the lock again and sat down on the toilet, which was as new as the rest of the room. The toilet faced some kind of African sculpture of a boy peeing. Great, we were going to watch each other. And we did.

My pants were down around my ankles, and I stared at my boots and took care of what I needed to take care of, and then I just sat there. I was the boy at the party who stays in the bathroom. And that's not cool. But Flan was here and even though I could say objectively that maybe she was too young to be at this type of party, I also sort of knew she was the coolest girl here. Maybe even cooler than Ruth, and that gave me a reason to stop being the boy in the bathroom. I reached around me, then, and tried to pull the handle. But instead there were buttons. So I pushed them.

The toilet flushed in near silence. I didn't move. Then there was a gushing noise and, well, something hit my ass. Something hot and wet. I shot forward the moment I felt that, because it was like nothing I'd ever felt before and it was totally freakish, and as I started to go forward, my new boots weren't able to get traction on that marble, and it was like I was getting shot into the air by a geyser at a hundred miles an hour toward that pissing African boy, thinking only one thought, *what the hell is happening to my ass?*

And since my balance was long gone, my head hit the boy's midsection. The sculpture was made of something surprisingly hard, like bronze. And he didn't move. Then everything went black.

"It can never be," Arno said to Liesel, for about the twentieth time. He was getting really bored of having to break up with her, but she just wasn't going away. They were in the living room on a couch, and Liesel was practically crouched over him, stroking his hair. He sat there, looking up at her.

Around them, the party was starting to fall apart. There was a couple fighting furiously in one corner and a bunch of seniors from Trinity in another, smoking pot and talking quietly about how they thought it was cool to be Republican. Some girls had passed out on the couch opposite Arno, and he looked vaguely under their skirts, but he felt so glum about the girl on top of him that he didn't even feel that sleazy about it.

"We are going to make this work," Liesel slurred. She puckered her lips at him and he knew she was about as good-looking as people get, but all he saw were the lips of a camel, about to slobber all over the side of his face.

"I'm sorry Liesel—you're just—you're too good for me."

"*Bullshit*," Liesel whispered, "*I'm never letting you go.*" She licked his ear. And inside, a voice said to him *you should've let her break up with you.* And he knew the voice was right, that if he'd just done nothing, she would have gone away, but he'd played the power card of ending it first and she wasn't going to let him get away with that. And obviously, the inner voice belonged to Jonathan. *She needs to be the one to walk away. Don't you know that?* Now wait a second, where the hell was Jonathan?

"Could you excuse me for a second?" Arno had to slide down onto the floor and actually crawl away from Liesel. The Trinity people laughed, and Arno did nothing to stop them. He straightened his pants and went into the kitchen. Mickey was in there. The ginger ale had run out, and now he was making tequila shots with Tabasco sauce and smoked oysters. Music continued to blast: Now it was "Ramblin' Man," by the Allman Brothers.

"You want one of these?" Mickey held up a shot glass filled with red liquid, the oyster bobbing in the middle of it.

"No, listen to me—" Arno said, watching Mickey slam back the shot as David wandered in. David had found a fisherman's hat with lures stuck in the brim and he was wearing it pulled low over his eyes. Somehow, Arno thought, it worked perfectly on him.

"Bleah!" Mickey screamed. But he didn't puke the shot.

"What's up?" David asked. He poured himself a glass of orange juice. They stood together, and a couple of girls and some guys he didn't know who probably went to Dwight all seemed to look to see what they'd do. Then Patch wandered in.

"This is fun," Patch said. He'd found a piece of chocolate mousse cake and he was eating it with some peppermint stick ice cream. He was always much more into dessert than drinking.

"Has anyone seen Jonathan?" Arno asked. The four of them looked at each other. It always, always felt weird when they were together and Jonathan wasn't there. And this was the third time in a week and a half that it had happened.

"I saw him go to the bathroom," one of the girls said. Arno looked at her. She was probably a sophomore, not really sure of herself yet. Those kinds always went for Jonathan.

"Which one?" Arno asked.

"I don't know," the girl was suddenly shy in front of all the guys looking at her. "Maybe I'm wrong." And

307

she disappeared into the living room. The four of them watched her go.

"How weird of him to disappear." Patch grinned. "I mean, isn't that *my* job?"

"He's been pretty depressed lately," David said.

"I think I heard that that Ruth girl doesn't even like him anymore," Arno said.

"Well what the hell? Let's go find him," Mickey said. But nobody moved.

"Did I tell you guys that my dad flew to London today to see Jonathan's dad?" Arno asked. Nobody said anything.

"You know why, right?" David asked.

"Something about money?" Arno said. He shook his head. Beyond that, he didn't have a clue. His dad and what he did was a mystery to him. Arno kind of knew he was gay, but he'd known that for so long that it was no longer a big deal to him.

"Well, I guess I have to say it: His dad stole money from all our parents. It was years ago, but I guess he wanted to come clean about it before marrying PISS," David said. "It's been freaking Jonathan out."

"I thought it was just that his Dad was getting remarried," Mickey said, "and that he had to pick one of us to go on the honeymoon."

"Wow," Arno said as he suddenly realized why his

parents had been acting like assholes that night and how awful Jonathan's time at his house must have been.

"I think he thinks we'd all hate him if we knew," David said, this time looking around at all of them.

"Because his dad's a dick?" Patch asked. He scratched his head. "My dad's a dick, and you guys don't hate me."

"It's different—your dad never stole anything. Where the hell do you think Jonathan is now?" Mickey asked.

"Hiding somewhere," David said. "Hopefully he didn't hop out a window—especially if Ruth broke up with him. I think I heard she did that."

"Well, Jonathan can get pretty dramatic," Arno said. "And if he lost a really cool girl and he thinks we all hate him . . ."

Then the four of them were tearing through the hallways of the gigantic Shulman apartment, looking for him. They passed little Flan Flood, who had her coat on and looked like she was leaving but who said she'd only seen Jonathan for a second. Patch paused for a second to ask if she was really supposed to be there, but then he stopped when he remembered what all of them had been doing in eighth grade and realized Flan was way more mature than most of the upperclassman there anyway. They pulled open the door to Ginger's bedroom and looked in, and it turned out she'd been in there for the entire party with the freshman from Yale who David had stuffed in the student/alumni game. After they said hello to her, they went through all the public rooms and checked all the bathrooms. No Jonathan.

Then everyone followed Arno down to the master bedroom. The door was locked. So they dragged Ginger Shulman out of bed and she yelled through the door. A girl nobody recognized opened it. She was in there with Adam Rickenbacher, who turned pale when he saw them all. But still no Jonathan.

"There's no key to the bathroom," Ginger said. "Try popping the lock with a credit card. Clean up whatever you find." And Ginger went back to her Yalie.

"Give him a minute to come out. He must've heard us," David said.

The four of them stood and looked at the blank door.

"Shhhh," Arno put his head to the wood. Silence and the sound of gushing water.

"Don't say it," David said.

"If he—"

"Pop the lock!" Patch yelled.

Then Mickey, who was good at that sort of thing, got down on his knees with an American Express

310

Platinum card. He popped the lock, but the door still didn't open.

"That's it!" Mickey screamed. "Launch me."

So Arno got on one side of Mickey and David got on the other. They threw Mickey at the door like a human battering ram. The door flew open and Mickey sailed through.

"OH NO!" Mickey yelled.

## mickey knows a dead man when he sees one

"He's dead!" Mickey screamed. He knocked the bronze pissing-boy out of the way and knelt in front of Jonathan.

"With his pants down," David noted.

The four of them stood around Jonathan. Mickey knelt and touched his neck. He was still warm. A thin stream of water shot from the toilet and sprinkled Jonathan's backside. The water had pooled around him, but it was by no means a flood.

"What the hell is that?" David stared at the water shooting from the toilet. Mickey slammed down the lid. "It's one of those brand-new toilets with the ass-cleaner in it. It works like a car wash. Everybody's getting them."

"Weird." David opened the lid, but the toilet had stopped spraying.

"I don't think he's dead." Patch felt Jonathan's pulse. "Nope. He just knocked himself out."

Mickey yanked up Jonathan's pants. Patch wet a

hand towel in the sink and put it over the ugly red bump on Jonathan's forehead. They got him to his feet.

"Ow," Jonathan said.

"See? Alive." Patch looked at the toilet, and then the pissing boy. "I get it."

"What?" Mickey asked.

"That warm jet of water on his ass. He must've felt it and shot forward, and then he knocked himself out on the pissing boy's penis."

"It's like a nightmare come to life," David said, stroking his chin. "Wait'll I tell my parents."

"No," Jonathan shook his head. He was leaning against the sink.

"Oh. Right, I won't."

Jonathan said, "I thought you guys—when I wasn't conscious, I was in this dream state and you guys hated me."

The four of them were quiet. Ten seconds passed.

"Well, we were saving your life while you were thinking that," Mickey said.

"I'd hope my best friends would do that for me. Even if they did probably figure out by now that my father is a thief who robbed all their parents blind." Jonathan's voice was thin.

Everyone stared at the spot on the floor where Jonathan had spent the last half hour. It looked hard and wet and cold.

"There's got to be an empty room around here somewhere," Arno said. "Let's go find it and talk."

"In here," Arno said. He stopped in what appeared to be a screening room, since it was just a bunch of unbelievably comfortable-looking brown velvet armchairs loosely set up in front of a plasma screen television that was hung on a wall above a fireplace.

There were five really good chairs. The walls were lined with Randall Oddy paintings from his pornographic period, but the lights were low, so only Arno noticed because he still had a soft spot for Kelli and sometimes wrote her e-mails that he never told anyone about. Mickey arranged the chairs in a circle. Suddenly there was a croaking, frog-like sound.

"Froggy?" Mickey asked. "Go pass out somewhere else, we need the room."

So Alan Ebershoff got up from where he'd been curled behind a chair and wandered out, and Arno had to face the wall for a second, since he'd pretty much destroyed Froggy's parents' bedroom the week before. And David faced the wall, too, since the last time he'd seen Froggy, he was in Amanda's bedroom. The group sat down.

"Shall we break the ice with some quarters?" Mickey asked. He got out a couple of cans of Tecate from the back pockets of his jeans. There was a round glass table in the middle of the room that was perfect for quarters, assuming you weren't too concerned about the glass getting nicked.

"I think we need to deal with what's been happening with Jonathan, about what he said in the bathroom, about his dad." Arno sat back and crossed his legs. Somehow, he always looked way older than the rest of them.

"So that's what it was all about?" Patch asked. "I'm pretty sure I've heard my dad joke on and off about the money that was stolen for at least the last few years."

"You knew?" Jonathan asked. Everyone looked at him. Jonathan's eyes were the color of eggnog.

"Well, now that I think about it, I did. But before this, I hadn't really been thinking about it."

"Wait, were any of you thinking about it?" Jonathan asked.

"Mostly you were," David said. "I knew, and I guess Patch did, and Mickey half-knew. But Arno didn't—not till today."

"I can't believe it," Jonathan said. "I thought if you guys knew, you'd like, excommunicate me."

"We might, but not because of that," Arno looked around at the group, and nodded at Jonathan's pointy boots. Mickey immediately reached forward and yanked them off. Jonathan had Comme des Garcons socks on underneath, in a horribly complex pattern of blue and green swirls.

"These shoes and socks have got to stop," Arno said.

Everyone seemed to agree on this, and that strengthened Arno's position. So Jonathan did nothing as Mickey tossed the shoes and socks into the hall, where Liza Komansky's friend Jane scooped them up and took them to a bedroom to try them on.

"There's more, though," David said.

"Yeah?" Everyone stared at Jonathan's feet. They were incredibly pale.

"Well, correct me if I'm wrong, guys," he said. "But I think the thing that really tweaked at us was that it seemed like you were holding back from us, but we're like . . . like a team, you know?"

"Dude." Arno threw a pillow at David. "You're so gay."

Jonathan looked down uncomfortably when Arno said that, because, of course, he knew full well that Arno's dad really was gay.

"No, that's right, what David said." Mickey nodded.

"You want me to share everything?" Jonathan asked.

"Yeah. We share everything. You should too," said Mickey.

"Okay. Ruth just broke up with me and I think it's partly because her parents are international lawyers and they heard about what an asshole my father is. She didn't exactly say that, but I'm pretty sure that was part of it."

"Ow," Mickey said.

"But there's more," Jonathan said. "I don't want to have secrets from you guys. Mickey, I think you've got to talk to your parents about what's going on with their marriage—I don't know if your mom is having an affair, but she might be. And your Dad, well, you need to talk to him about whether he's having an affair, too. And David, your dad is crazy and must be stopped. And Arno, you need to talk to your dad about who he really is, and check in with your mom, too, about the affair thing."

Everyone was quiet then. Jonathan frowned. Then he said, "There's stuff I saw and heard when I was in your houses. I've got to tell you about it, what I just said is only the beginning. I don't want to keep this all inside anymore."

While all this was going on, Patch had gotten hold

of a universal remote. He'd turned on the television and begun to watch *Butch Cassidy and the Sundance Kid.* In the midst of the shocked silence, Patch belly-laughed, loudly, while Paul Newman and Robert Redford bicycled happily around in nature. Everyone watched quietly, listening not to the movie but to the new silence between them, knowing that if they wanted to, they could learn all sorts of stuff they might have long preferred not to know.

"Maybe you don't need to hear all of it," Jonathan said.

"Maybe not," Patch said, turning off the TV.

"Well, okay. Thanks for getting me out of that bathroom, and for hopefully not telling anybody about it." Jonathan rubbed his head. "I hope this bump goes away before my mom gets home."

"Oh wow," Arno said. "Tomorrow is Thanksgiving."

Jonathan stood up and looked out the window. He said, "My mom promised she'd be home to cook a turkey. And she'd better be. This being on my own is obviously more than I can handle."

"Well no matter what, you can come over to my house if she's late or something," Arno said.

"Thanks," Jonathan said, and Arno stared at him, because Jonathan didn't sound sarcastic at all. He sounded like he really meant it. "And guys?"

"Yeah?"

"I'll figure out this Caribbean thing. I'm not sure I can handle it without you all, anyway."

## david gets some more of that newfangled grobart philosophy

David wasn't that bombed, but he was having trouble getting his key to fit in his front door. It seemed too big, and then too small.

Then the door opened and his father stood staring at him, in his pajamas, and he was both too big and too small, too. David wondered if he might be Alice and if this was the looking glass. But when he looked down, he wasn't wearing white shoes and a blue dress with a big white bow around the middle. He was grateful for that, at least.

"Come and sit with me in the living room." His father turned and padded down the quiet corridor and David followed. The house was terribly quiet and smelled of roast chicken, as usual.

"Everything work out okay with Jonathan? I ask because I've got a session with his mom tomorrow, right before we stuff the turkey, and I need all the help I can get."

"Dad?"

"Yes?"

David shifted and pulled a thick copy of the American Psychoanalytic Institute's monthly newsletter out from under his butt.

"Are you sure that telling so many secrets is such a good idea? 'Cause I'm kind of thinking it causes a lot of trouble when you do that."

"Oh no, I'm absolutely sure it's the right thing. I've been in this game a long time and the thing I know is that when a marriage is breaking up or a man is cheating on a woman, everyone ought to know all about all the details, so they can set to work hashing it out."

"I don't know," David said. "I'm thinking those situations are delicate, you know?"

Then of course Sam Grobart launched into a long, complex set of reasons that clarified why David was wrong, but David tuned him out. He glanced around the book-strewn room and wondered why his dad was always wandering around in the middle of the night when his mom was asleep. Then his phone rang once, and stopped. David glanced at the screen. Amanda.

Meanwhile, his dad continued to ramble on about secrets and how people should give them up faster than a dollar to a beggar on the subway. And David thought, I definitely need to call Amanda. Right now.

"I need to make a call." David went down to the street to call from there, because he was realizing that if his dad didn't believe in secrets, then nothing in his house could be truly private. So he took the elevator down to the lobby and stepped outside.

There, in the back of a black car, was Amanda. He walked over as the window went down, and looked in at her. She was alone.

"I'm just coming back from Ginger's." Amanda's voice was low and calm. "My parent's are already in Sagaponack. I was going to stay home alone tonight."

The door to the black car opened. David looked back at his building, which seemed far less warm and inviting than this car.

"But we're not going to get engaged. I don't think that makes any sense," David said, once he'd settled himself in the seat next to her.

"You're right. It's just taken me a long time to deal with the fact that someone as cool as you could like someone like me."

"Are you serious?" David asked, realizing this was exactly the sort of reason his father would use to explain why Amanda had often been so awful to him.

"I know," Amanda said, quietly. "It's crazy isn't it? But it's true."

And they drove the few blocks to her house in

complete make-out mode, with no regard for the driver, which was okay, because he was talking loudly on the phone to a cousin in eastern Pennsylvania about how to make the cranberry sauce for that night's Thanksgiving dinner.

David and Amanda went into her house, and then into her bedroom, where David had had such a terrible moment only a few days earlier. They ended up on her bed.

"It's so good to be together again." David felt the tiny cuteness of Amanda and realized what he'd said was true. And Amanda, who had been so mean to David so many times, just squeezed him around the neck like she really didn't want to lose him again. And that felt really good, to both of them.

## my mom comes through on her promise

"What happened to your forehead?" my mom asked.

Obviously I didn't want to explain that the bruise on my forehead had come from when I'd inadvertently knocked myself unconscious on a bronze penis, so I said: "I was staying at Mickey's and the bed they built me went crazy and smashed me into the ceiling." I shrugged. The bed story was almost true.

"I see. Billy was just telling me he had some very nice talks with you." She nodded to Billy, who was wearing a pair of my favorite Rogan jeans and one of my Polo shirts.

We were standing in a corner of the kitchen, next to a wall where Billy had painted a bunch of bears wearing party hats, who were cavorting around a fountain. My mom seemed to like the bears. And she clearly liked Billy. I shook my head. Life was not becoming less bizarre.

"Sure," I said. Part of me had been wanting to say that I hadn't much enjoyed how Billy had screwed up my clothes and our apartment, but I figured my mom would just see all that, now that she was back. Nope. Wrong.

"We're not selling the apartment, are we?'

"No way," my mother said. "We could never sell this place with it painted the way it is. This sort of thing frightens people! We're going to stay right here."

She raised an eyebrow at me and I finally got it. The insane painting had been part of a bigger plan—no matter how much trouble my dad got into, my mom was tough and wacky and didn't care if people talked about her ex-husband being a thief or the weird bears that were painted on her walls. And all this meant that we definitely weren't going to be moving to Brooklyn and I could keep my room and my friends, and with the exception of a few restaurants that were owned by my dad's former clients, I wouldn't have to hide my face at all and could still go to all the cool places I always had.

"What are we going to do for dinner?" I asked. It was, after all, Thanksgiving. And I had to give my mom that, she'd made it back in time.

"I thought we'd take Billy and go to Aquavit. I know it's not traditional, but they're holding a table for us, and I love the gravlax."

I smiled, because the deal was not that my mom make a traditional Thanksgiving, just that she actually be around for it. It was kind of like with my friends. We all didn't have to be perfect, but we had to be there for each other anyway.

My mom went to the living room and got on the phone to call my brother, who was having Thanksgiving with his girlfriend's family in L.A. I stood there in the kitchen with Billy and I just had to ask. "Are you having an affair with Lucy Pardo?"

Billy turned to me. He had that same warm smile I associated with Patch, but lurking behind his smile were a few more years of life, so he was not so easy to read.

"Not really."

"What kind of answer is that?"

"Do you really want to know the truth?"

"Um."

"Jonathan, get on the phone." My mother strode into the room and smiled at me and Billy. And that's when I knew that she was well aware of Billy and Lucy Pardo.

"Are you on with Ted?" I asked.

"No. It's your father." My mother shoved the phone at me. So I took it.

"Hi." I knew my voice sounded awfully soft and weak. It was difficult for me to know what I should and shouldn't say. Then my dad said, "I hope my bad moves in life haven't affected your life too much."

Which was the opening I was looking for.

"Well, they have!"

"How?"

Right then I remembered how beyond all else, my dad was able to listen. He was way better than David's dad at doing that, who was supposed to listen professionally.

"Because I've been really embarrassed!"

"Your friends were rough on you?"

"Actually—" Then I had to stop. Because they hadn't been so rough on me. But still. Right? And I could hear my dad, so far away on the phone. And he was quiet and he was listening.

"Dad? I'd really like to bring them all on this sailing trip. I can't choose just one, and really, we're all like ten times better together than we are apart."

"Okay."

"Just like that, okay?"

"Just like that."

We kept talking for a while, because he was my father, and honestly, how could I not? He was a good guy. I mean, he'd screwed up, but I got the feeling he was trying to make it right, and what else could I really ask of him? I didn't ask about what happened with Arno's dad, though. I just figured that whatever deal they'd made with each other wasn't my problem.

Later, when I was off the phone, I wandered into the living room. My mom was there, talking with Billy and admiring some vines of roses he'd painted between the windows, where a Richard Avedon photograph of my mother that was taken in the seventies used to be.

I came up to them and tried to let them know I was there. I was now totally against ever being caught again in a position where I could hear something someone was saying when they didn't want me to hear it.

"I think you're doing a terrific job. Really first rate. But let's be honest. You're not done."

"Right," Billy smiled.

"So I'd like you to keep living here, in

Jonathan's brother's room. Keep painting. I like a busy house."

"Don't I—" but then I quieted down. I'd be away in the Caribbean in just a few weeks anyway, and even though Billy had ruined a bunch of my coolest clothes, I had to admit that I liked that guy.

"What do you think, Jonathan?" Billy asked.

"It's fine with me, but the new official house rule is you keep your hands off my clothes and . . . well I guess that's it."

Mickey stood up from the table. His family was having Thanksgiving dinner with the Fradys in a private room at Soho House. Month to month, the Pardos and the Frady family could barely keep track of whether they were getting along, much less whether Mickey and Philippa Frady were still together. But Thanksgiving together remained a staple of each year, as consistent as Jackson Frady's death-ray glare for Mickey.

"*Let's go have a drink at the bar downstairs,*" Mickey whispered to Philippa, who was working hard to avoid dealing with the fact that she was sitting next to him. "*Please?*"

"Fine," she said. She was dressed in a brown cocktail dress with lots of pleats and a pair of pink shoes. Her hair was down and she looked both extremely beautiful and unbelievably bored.

They walked together down the main staircase. When they got to the bar, which was outfitted with white leather seats and a zinc bartop, they sat down at one end, and the bartenders paid no attention because the newly crowned editor of *Vogue* was at the other end of the bar with her family, and they were drinking mulled wine and waiting to go up to their own Thanksgiving table.

"I love you," Mickey said. "We just went through some real craziness with Jonathan, where he was trying to hide what was going on with him, but we figured it out and what that made me realize was that—"

"You love me?"

"Yes."

They smiled at each other. Mickey slipped off his barstool and stood in front of Philippa. He came forward. She opened her arms. They embraced.

"I don't really see how this is connected to Jonathan—except I heard he tried to drown himself in a toilet."

"That's not true. Anyway, I don't get it either," Mickey smiled. "But whatever happened with him, it made me realize that you're like, my destiny."

"It's scary when you use words like that."

She leaned against the bar and stared into Mickey's eyes. He wasn't high or anything. He'd left the Triumph at home and wasn't trying to get into any trouble just now. Though of course he would later, when everyone met up either at Man Ray or Lucky Strike.

"We're too young for the intensity of this feeling. I've told you. I don't want to be Romeo and Juliet."

"Don't tell me we can't go out." Mickey fell forward slightly, so she'd hold him up. The warmth between their bodies seemed to expand, to surround them.

Then the bartender came by, but he saw he didn't need to ask them for their drink order, not right now. And there was music too, the new Yo La Tengo, which sounded like a rainstorm.

"How about we make a pact?"

"Sure." Mickey nodded. "And then let's leave. We'll go up there and both say we feel very tired and they'll let us go home."

"They won't."

"If we yawn a lot they will."

Philippa nodded. Her brown eyes glittered. "If we both end up at Brown, we can be really in love and like, live off campus in our apartment together and throw dinner parties."

"But not till then."

"Not till then."

Mickey shook his head. Of course they'd find themselves at Brown together, but this seemed so outrageous, this . . . *waiting*.

"We can see other people till then," Philippa said.

"No."

"Or no pact at all."

"Our love is going to make me waste away and die," Mickey said. But he said yes. They would have this pact. He'd done far stranger things and he loved her so much. Philippa went upstairs to tell their parents they were leaving together, even though they weren't going out.

Mickey stood outside and waited for Philippa. He said hello to the doorman, who was called Paul. Then an English guy drove up on a black BMW motorcycle and parked on the sidewalk. He tossed the keys to the doorman and swept through the front door without saying a word.

"Asshole, huh?" Mickey nodded at the English guy's back. The doorman looked, too.

"Yeah. He expects me to go park his bike and he doesn't even tip me."

"I'll give you a hundred bucks if you let me go park it."

"Done."

"Cool." Mickey slipped him the bill and hopped on the big bike. Then Philippa came out.

"No way," she said.

"If we're going to have a pact, then I'm going to have fun—and the fun starts with, um, *parking* this bike. Now, hop on."

Philippa shook her head, but then she did get on and they roared off into the darkness.

"Hey, the parking lot is the other way," the doorman said to the wind, and smiled to himself.

## arno already knew the bad news

Arno sat in his living room with his parents. They were picking at a plate of aged smelly cheese. The house was warm and there was a Bach cantata playing low, and because the speakers were hidden in places where nobody could see them and, subsequently, nobody could remember where they were, the house felt haunted with the music.

"The truth is it's been this way for a long time," Allie said to her son. They sat together on a low couch. Alec, Arno's dad, paced in front of them. As usual, he was dressed in an impossibly well-cut blue suit. He was frowning and he had a glass of champagne that he sipped from occasionally. Arno and Allie had glasses too, but they weren't drinking.

"I think I already knew," Arno said. "But it was really weird having to hear it from Jonathan at a party at three o'clock in the morning."

"Sorry about that," Alec said. "We have had what was called, in very different times than these, a marriage of convenience, and clearly it's wildly outdated. We've tried everything—as you saw just a few weeks ago in Miami. Nothing works, so now we will extract ourselves from each other, but neither of us will come apart from you, if you see what I mean."

"I guess." Arno sighed and cut himself a piece of the blue-streaked Royal Stilton. To Arno, it just sounded like they were going to go on as before.

"But we're going to officially divorce."

That got Arno's attention. He looked up at his father.

"If you're going to make me go to therapy because of this, one thing you ought to know is that I absolutely refuse to go to David's dad. That guy is bonkers."

"I'm going to stop seeing him too," Allie said.

"Will you also stop seeing Mickey's dad?" Arno asked, quickly. But Allie only stared at the river of antique rug that covered the great length of the living room floor.

"I don't know about her, but you can be assured that *I* will," Alec said, "but we will continue to represent and sell his work, so maybe that's not even true." And then Alec sat down, suddenly, in a chair across from his wife and son.

"This is hard," Alec said. "Really hard. This will take some time."

And after a few minutes of silence, the three Wildenburgers got up and went into the dining room to have Thanksgiving dinner with their fifteen guests, who had been sitting there the entire time waiting for them and whispering about all they knew that could be the matter. Alec took his place at one end of the long table and Allie sat down at the other end, and the Thanksgiving dinner began with the guests chattering at each other in German and Swiss and Italian about what would happen to the great Wildenburger art dynasty now that the troubles on the domestic front could no longer be hidden.

Arno, meanwhile, ate a bit of turkey and then got up from the table and went to make some phone calls. Everyone had agreed to meet at Man Ray at ten if not before, since everyone had also agreed that the real home was wherever the other four guys were, and certainly not among all the squabbling adults.

**if there's a sunset, who do you think is headed off into it?**

At the last minute, the Flood family had decided to have Thanksgiving in New York rather than in Greenwich. Nobody could find February, and that was so unusual that they all wanted to be near home in case she returned from wherever she was. All the Floods were equipped with cell phones and pagers, since it was one thing for Patch to disappear, but February? That meant trouble.

Frederick and Fiona Flood had taken over the kitchen, along with a housekeeper and a cook, and they'd begun to make dinner. All this activity had prompted Patch to go horseback riding in Central Park with Flan.

Patch and Flan had had a great time, cantering down the paths and chasing pigeons and the one bald eagle that was known to roost near the Alice in Wonderland sculpture. And when they were done, they'd driven around in the yellow Mercedes for a while, not even talking, just listening to Flan's new Fiona Apple CD on the stereo and enjoying a New York that was nearly emptied of people now that the Macy's Thanksgiving Day parade had ended and everyone was back home getting ready to tuck into some turkey.

Eventually, Patch pulled up in front of the Floods' house and idled the car.

"That was fun," Patch said. "Flan, you're a cool girl. So long as you don't grow up too fast."

"That's funny, I feel the opposite about you," Flan said, as she hopped out of the car. "You're a cool guy, so long as you remember to grow up a little. Now listen, remember, all you're supposed to do is drive to the garage and leave the car there, and then come home for Thanksgiving dinner."

"I know. We just talked about this five minutes ago."

But Flan didn't move. She looked searchingly at her big brother. On Perry Street, leaves swirled down around them. It was just beginning to get dark.

"Promise me you'll come home."

There was quiet between them. Patch smiled his golden smile at his beautiful little sister.

"Go in and tell mom and dad not to wait—get started without me."

Flan set her jaw then, and turned quickly from her big brother. It was as if somehow she understood him, that his destiny was not necessarily to always be at dinner, to say the least. But before she went in the house, Patch called out the window to her.

"Yeah?" Flan cocked her head.

"It's okay with me if you go out with Jonathan. I mean, I think you should."

And Flan smiled, because it was always weird when her brother knew more than anyone thought and could see things other people couldn't.

Patch waved at her, and drove down the street. When he got to Seventh Avenue, he turned right. The garage was down here somewhere. Of course he knew where. He'd been driving there with his parents since he was like, one. But suddenly, he passed it. He knew he had, but the leaves were so nice on the trees as he turned right and went back into the West Village, and then left onto the West Side Highway, in order, he thought, to simply catch one last glimpse of the failing light.

He turned off the music and just listened to the quiet city. The sun began to set to his left, over New Jersey, beyond the water. And it felt so right to just . . . keep going north, toward upstate, and then maybe west, out of town. He wasn't sure yet. He'd have to see. Just keep going.

**all of us together again**

I sat in the middle of a booth in the back of Man Ray with David, and Mickey, and Arno. It was just before midnight and Thanksgiving was definitely over. We were all drinking Stellas and generally being relieved that we'd made it through dinner with our families. And then I tapped my glass with my knife, which was something annoying that only our parents ever did, and said I had an announcement to make.

"I talked to my Dad and you are all invited on the honeymoon. And Patch, too, if we can find him before then."

Everyone cheered and I kept talking. "Because I know this sounds cheesy, but the last week and a half has made me realize that I really need you guys and I think we all need each other."

Arno started laughing first, but pretty soon they all were.

"Dude, that is so cheesy, but yeah, you're

right." David threw his arm around my neck and mussed my hair. I spilled a little beer on my new olive G-Star cargo pants that I was trying to break in for the trip, but I didn't care too much since Billy had broken me of being quite so uptight about my clothes.

"Hell," Mickey said. "Better to be a cheeseball than to say, get caught in an Upper West Side bathroom with your pants down and a bronze penis-boy standing over you!"

I touched the bruise on the side of my forehead.

"Oh, I'm sorry—that happened to you, didn't it?" Mickey snorted.

"Yeah."

My friends were laughing, hard. David had tears running down his cheeks and Mickey was banging his head on the table. Arno was laughing too, but not as hard.

"Everything go okay with your family?" I asked.

"No," Arno said. "Not at all. But we're going to figure it out. One thing's for sure, I can't wait for us to be seniors and then head off to college, because this living at home is really hard."

"Well, it's not like we live at home in any

normal kind of way," I said.

"I know. That's what's hard."

"My dad says that's a problem." David caught his breath from the giggles and sipped at his glass of Stella.

"Your dad . . . " I trailed off.

"I know, I know. I definitely won't be sharing much with him anymore—especially not about you guys, or me and Amanda."

"You two got back together?" Mickey asked.

David nodded a guilty yes.

"She's getting comfortable with how cool I am," David said. And everyone just stared in shock, and tried not to laugh. Because of course the only person who thought David was *that* cool was Amanda.

"What'd Philippa say, anyway?" David asked Mickey, suddenly.

"Just that she acknowledged that we're totally in love but we can't ever really go out unless we end up at Brown together. But I took her on a motorcycle ride she won't forget, and then we shot the bike off a pier into the East River, and we made out for a while, even though yeah, we're over."

So that relationship wasn't going away, either.

Then everybody turned to Arno.

"Don't worry about it. I'm definitely done with Liesel." Arno shook his thick black hair back and forth. "Definitely."

"Then what's she doing here?" I asked. And all of us looked, and sure enough, Liesel and Ruth and some girls I didn't know were headed right toward us. One of the girls came right up to our table. It was Selina Trieff.

"Have you seen Patch?" she asked. Of course Ruth wouldn't meet my eyes because she'd broken up with me only the night before.

"Not since the weekend," Mickey said. "You should call Flan and ask her."

"Yeah," Selina said. "That's a good idea."

I'd looked away when she mentioned Flan. And all of a sudden I realized I didn't want to see Ruth at all. I wanted Flan.

"Wait, I'll call Flan," I said. "I've been meaning to do that anyway."

I shifted my phone out of my pants pocket and dialed Flan's number. The phone started to ring.

Then they all joined us, and suddenly our booth was very crowded and loud. And Selina was talking to Arno, and suddenly she didn't seem as worried about where Patch was.

"Excuse me for a second," I said. And Ruth didn't seem to want to look at me, which was okay, because I didn't really want to look at her, either. It had been a fun crush, but I realized that the whole time with Ruth, I never really stopped comparing her to Flan. And even I got what that meant.

"Hello?" Flan said.

"What are you doing?"

"Um, nothing. Eating leftover turkey and watching TV."

"Well, can I come over and hang out?"

"Sure," Flan said. "Actually, I've been wondering when you were going to call."